Crossing The Line

COREY BRYANT

Contents

Prologue

"Jacorius and all of his women!" said Lashawn to herself, as she sat back and evaluated the situation. Her situation, "Then Jacorius is a hustler, he ain't fooling me!" thought Lashawn to herself. "A thug! I can't get involved with nobody like that! A street nigga. Especially with the job I got." Then at the same time in her heart she always wanted a street nigga. A strong man but with some sense. And it wouldn't hurt if he was a drug dealer, Even though she's always done for herself like she was raised to do. But every woman wanted to be spoiled every now and then. All of a sudden from somewhere in her psyche that reoccurring fantasy came to surface: same guy, same washroom in the back of her parents' house when she was 17 or 18. "I told you my mother was up in the front of the house!" Before she knew it, the thug had his hand around her butt in a rough kind of way. He pulls Lashawn up on his hard dick. Pausing for a moment, as he look Lashawn in the eyes, he started kissing her! Slow and deep. With her only putting up a slight resistance before returning the kisses, just as deep, hard and passionate.

Moaning as they kissed, and her moans were exciting this thug, making him pick her up and put her on the washing machine and commenced to pull her tube shirt over her head exposing her breasts and started hungrily sucking them. "Lashawn... Lashawn!" said Anita the waitress, snapping Lashawn out of her fantasy from when she was a teenager.

Chapter 1

WORK DETAIL THINGS

Jacorious, Malik, and Johnny were loading the truck up, with weed eaters blowers, rakes and hoes. They were the ground men at Bethune, Cook College in Daytona Beach, Florida. Johnny was the supervisor over the grounds, in charge of keeping the campus looking pretty and groomed. Jacorius and Malik were incarcerated at a minimum security prison, for good behavior. They were allowed to come out and work for the college at a rate of 25 cents an hour. Adds up to about $40 a month. Jacorious nor Malik cared about the little money they were being paid, because both of them have been incarcerated long time, so they were content with being able to come out and work with a cool boss man like Johnny. Johnny would let them have cell phones, meet up with women to have sex or whatever. That was what inmates called a "sweet job." Jacorius had been incarcerated for about 15 years for murder and Malik had been incarcerated for 10 years. Jacorius was more of the laid-back gangster/hustler type of guy.

Whereas Malik was more of a laid-back Playboy type of guy. A pretty boy, but slick with the women. Johnny their boss man was an old school player / playboy himself. His hair was long like a pimp in the '70s and he loved women, music and beer. "Y'all ready?" Asked Johnny. "Yeah, let's roll." Said Jacorius as they hopped in the truck. As soon as they were putting pulling off Jacorius and Malik pulled out their phones and were checking their messages.

"Y'all want to go to Greg's to get some breakfast? "Asked Johnny. "Yeah. That's the spot where they sell the pink salmon and stuff." Yeah.. We ain't been over there in a while." Said Johnny, as he drove the old red Ram off the campus. This was a ritual, for the three, most of the time. After they do there rounds of picking up paper, around the campus. It was another crew of four grounds men, but Johnny kept his two with him. They all got along, works good together and all had common goals and desires when it came to work. And that was to try and fuck many of the females there! Mostly staff! The real grown ups! Some of the older students, that might have quit going when they were younger, due to some of life circumstances. Or just chose to go when they got older. A lot of them was going to night classes. By the time they started coming to class, Jacorius, Malik, and the other inmates were about to go back to the minimum security prison they were housed at. It didn't make these Guys no difference, because they were running across females everywhere! Sometimes they got lucky and get chosen without even saying much. And sometimes they were straight pulling females at places they went with Johnny. Malik mostly! He was getting chose a lot! He was a light brown skin dude with light brown eyes. Handsome, and in shape, like an exercise instructor, but not that beefed up.

So, women were choosing him especially when they recognize he was actually incarcerated. But he mostly was focused on money! He was more of a drug dealing hustler. So he was trying to link up with other hustlers who were on the outside, to get plugged in! He wanted to do right, but circumstances with his family finances, awoken a desire to do what he knows best, that was to hustle! So his point of view, was any female he runs into and wanted to kick it with him, she also had to be already straight financially, or was about the hustle one way or the other. He had a few he had ran into from around his way, outside of Daytona Beach. Not many though, because he had been incarcerated so long that they basically have forgotten about him! That wasn't a much of a problem, because he had game, and understood the power of his self-personal magnetism and was strikingly handsome. Jacorius, Wasn't a slouch! He was light-skinned, short, stood about 5-8, kind of Stocky Built, you can tell that he worked out. Naturally had the gift to Gab, so when encounters with women occurred, he was ready! On the other hand, Jacorius was yearning to get chosen by the right woman. He didn't know what had him with such contradictory inner feelings! Was it a primal want and desire? Or was it his vulnerability, due to being incarcerated so long? Did that fact, have him searching for his soulmate on the low? As they rode to the restaurant, Jacorius was strolling through Facebook, looking at females he knew from back in the school days.

Tripping off some of their appearances and how they've changed and how some of them hadn't changed. "Damn! Chaprel still fine as fuck!" Said Jacorius, to no one in particular. "Let me see her!" Said Johnny. Jacorius Handed Johnny the phone, as they pulled into to the parking lot of Greg's, the breakfast restaurant.! "Umm uh!" Said Johnny. Jay that girl finer I than cat hair! How old you say she was?" Jacorius and Malik laughed at that Johnny's comment. "She my age 34." "Let me see what all the fuss is about!" Said Malik. Johnny look back down at the photo one more good time before he passes the phone to Malik. "Damn! She is finer than cat hair! Is she married?" "I don't think so." Said Jacorius, as he looks back at the photo. Jacorius sent Chaprel a message through messenger. {Looking good! Are you married? } What ya'll want?" Asked Johnny has he got out of the truck. "I want my usual, the Salmon breakfast, with the cheese eggs, and grits." "I'll get the same thing Johnny. Get me an orange used to go with it." Said Malik. Oh yeah, I forgot, get me an apple juice." Said Jacorius, as he handed Johnny his money. If I were you Jay, I would be trying to get ole girl! What's her name? Chaprel?" "Yeah. I am just got in her inbox said Jacorius. Hell yea! You supposed to! Get her to come see you, put that money on the book! Get her down here, get a room and fuck that fine motherfucker! Said Malik.

They laughed and gave each other dap in agreement. after 5-10 minutes Johnny returned with their plates and they left and went to one of their favorite spots to chill, and that's in an old parking deck on campus. It had a security code to get into the gate part, and on the side there was a parking lot in which was hardly ever used. They sat there ate and talked. Jacorius was Back on the phone with his mother, which was a morning routine and he would smoke him a joint, Then and during the time he's walking, picking up paper, during his morning route. They were about to get started on a project, and Jacorius had got a text from a female name Dee-Dee. His play cuz. He called her his play cuz because, that was what she had told her boyfriend Kurt, who was locked up with him, for a brief moment at another prison. It was funny how they connected. A case of, you can't trust just anybody! Well, in this situation, it was an honest, play for an honor underplay. Jacorius transferred, from a camp in South Bay, to Polk City, and Kurt was there. Kurt and Jacorius,Was cool. they used to hang on the same block together, when they were young. Kurt had just got locked up, and Jacorius had been bidding. They hadn't seen or talked to each other in all of those years, so they stayed talking and catching up. Kurt told his girl Dee-dee that Jacorius was there, and she immediately told Kurt that her and Jacorius was cousins and that she wanted to see him! Jacorius was walking through the dorm, that Kurt slept in that's when" when Kurt told him about him and Dee-Dee's conversation.

What's up Jay"! "What up my nigga!??" "I just got off the phone with my ole lady, Dee- Dee. I told her you were here and she screamed!" "Screamed?" Asked Jacorius, looking kind of surprised. "Yeah. She said ya'll were sum kin!" For some reason, Jacorius went right along with Dee-Dee. He didn't know whether they were cousins or not! "Yeah, yeah. We are! But I'm not sure how." Said Jacorius, being careful on how he should respond. "She said her grandmama was a Jackson like y'all. Said your great-granddaddy and her great-grandmother were sister and brother or something like that." "Oh! I think so!" said Jacorius. "Yeah, but anyway she wants to see you if you're getting a visit this weekend." "Oh okay! Shit, I supposed to be out there this weekend, so I see her then." Said Jacorius. Somewhat getting excited, on the low. As he was walking off from Kurt, he was thinking to himself: "Why am I getting excited? Especially about one of the one of my homies girl? I need to get my own girl?!" Said Jacorius to himself. But nevertheless, he was ready to see Dee- Dee!

Chapter 2

WEEKEND VISIT

That weekend, just like clockwork, Dee- Dee was there! Visiting Kurt. Jacorius's mother and sister was there. They all sat together and ate and talked. Dee-dee appeared to be genuinely excited to see Jacorius, as they greet each other with a hug. The whole visit DeeDee was eyeing Jacorius. When she stood up, Jacorius was amazed that how fine Dee-dee had gotten with age. His mind was in overtime! Because She was watching him closely the whole visit. Dee-dee was still a stripper! She stood about 5'9', peanut butter brown skin. And at her age,still fine, and had younger stripper friends. After that visit, she told Kurt to get Jacorius address. She wanted to stay in touch, and in touch she did! When Jacorius transferred to a lower security camp, he wrote her and let her know and she wrote right back with her phone number! And from that point they communicated quite regularly. Dee-dee revealed all type of information about her hustle and how she would put Jacorius on as their manager once he gets out,Soon. So he was down with the plan! Jacorius was texting Dee-Dee back. {Good morning to you too.} Jacorius got into the truck with Johnny and they rode to an area on campus where they were starting that morning. It was close to the office of human resources. Plenty of sexy females worked in that building! Matter of fact that's in all the buildings! Near that building was the marketing and communications office.

True enough that building had a lot of women in it, but it was one in particular that had Jacorius attention. Her name was Lashawn. She was a couple of years older than Jacorius, but she was his kind of hype! She was she was a kind of small woman. Stood about five two or five three, brown skin, small frame woman, with a fine shape! With a down to earth, bubbly personality. Lashawn was an office manager, in the IT department. He seen her almost every day, when she would leave her office for lunch. She would meet up with some more fine women from different buildings at the food court. A couple of them were metermaids, which were also some sexy black women. One in particular, the youngest out of the bunch, Tanithia! Little waist,big round ass, pretty face,All the way with it! She had chose Malik so, he was sneaking out fucking her every now and then. Johnny and his men had to go through the food court all day every day, because they had a break room and supplies down in the basement of that building, so that was the perfect for Jacorius, wanting to see Lashawn. "Yo Jay." "What's up Johnny?" There go Lashawn!" We was just about to start cutting grass when Lashawn came out of her building heading to her car. "How you doing?!" "How are you this morning?" "I'm good! Especially now that I've seen you!" "Oh really?! "Said Lashawn, in her usual flirty but coated with being bubbly way.

"So, what is it about me that just brightens your day?" Asked Lashawn. "Let me see! Where do you want me to start at? Oh.. It's the smile for starters!" LaShawn laughed at Jacorius comment while opening her car door. "And I can't forget about that bubbly and down the earth personality." "Yeah I do have a bubbly personality! I believe I get that from my grandma! Laughed Lashawn, as she closed the door to her car and headed back to her building. "Well, I'm glad to be of some help, with lightning up your day!" "Well you're highly appreciated Lashawn! You have a nice day!" "You too!" Said Lashawn. Lashawn pulled off and Jacorius was watching her as she drove off. "Gotta have her!" Said Jacorius, as he crank his weed eater and got to work.

Chapter 3

Dope Chic

Lunch hour had done rolled around. Jacorius was in the basement with the rest of the crew minus Malik, having lunch. Jacorius had got through eating, and was sitting on the back stairway, by the exit door, looking at his phone. Specifically, Facebook as he puffed on a blunt. "Yo! Jay! Where you at?" Yelled Malik, as he entered the basement from the main hall stairs. "Yo! What's up! I'm on the back stairs!" Said Jacorius, while coughing on the weed he was smoking. "Oh I hear you, and smell you!" Laughed Malik. He ran up the stairs to Where Jacorius was sitting. "Hey man! You need to put that shit down and come get at this dope chic!" "Dope chic?!" Repeated Jacorius, as he looks from his phone to Malik. "Yeah! Dope bitch! Redbone gold grill! Long ass pretty nails, with jewels in them! A couple of gold and diamond chains and bracelets. Her whole persona says dope dealing bitch or my man a big dope dealer! I peep the car she got out of. A new charger!" "Oh yeah?" "Hell yeah nigga! Don't be procrastinating!

She's just your speed! I wanted to get her but I kick it with her friend Janelle! They take a few classes together. But they're up there in the food court. She told me to find her a nigga in prison since her friend got one!" Said Malik. "You cappin bro!" Said Jacorius, as headed down the stairs. "Cappin? Why would i do that? She specifically said one of these niggas working out here with us! Look at them niggas bro! She is talking about you! You got that dope boy/street nigga demeanor she likes. Let's go up there and catch them before they go to class at 3:30."

Malik and Jacorius climbed the stairs in no time to leave the basement and headed to the food court. "Glad we some workout type of niggas. Because those stairs got me breathing like a mother fucker! Shawty better be worth it!" Said Jacorius, as they walked down the hallway. "Nigga. When you see this red ass woman, nigga you going to be ready to go do a full workout!" laughed Malik. Jacorius put a piece of gum in his mouth, as they were walking down through the food court. "Look! There she is sitting at the corner table in the back. That chic she is sitting with, that's my girl!" "Yeah, I see her! Damn! She looks good as fuck from here!" I told you, my nigga! Let's go over there and put it down." Said Malik. The two smoothly approached the two women at the table. "What's up ladies! This my partner I was telling you about, Jay." Jacorius i mean! Jacorius,This is Niecy." "Nice to meet you Niecy!" Said Jacorius ,as he shook her hand. "Nice to meet you too!" Said Niecy. It was evident that Niecy was feeling Jacorius. She was smiling ear to ear showing all the shiny golds, in her mouth. And Jay, this is my girl Janelle, Janelle this is Jay!" "Nice to meet you Janelle!" "Likewise!" Said Janelle. "Give me your number." said Niecy, not wasting any time. "386-748-3490." obliged Jacorius. "Okay. I got you locked in, I'm about to text you. So you can lock my number in." "Okay! That's the move! Let's go! Oh it's nice meeting you Niecy And Jeneal!" "Nice meeting you too!" said Niecy And Janeal. Jacorius and Malik, walked off, heading back to the basement. "Oh yeah? You think so?" Asks Jacorius. He was on the phone with Niecy, prepared to put his phone up, and his secret hide place.

"Yeah, I think you fine nigga!" Laughed Niecy. "It's just, this is new to me! I've never dealt with a nigga locked up, besides my husband." "Oh you're married? And he's been to prison?" "Yeah! But we're on bad terms and shit. You might know him; his name is Big Doe." "Big Doe?" Repeated Jacorius. "Brown skin chubby, loudmouth, older nigga!" "Yeah that's him!" Laughs Niecy. "Yeah I know!" Laughed Jacorius. But check this out. We're about to go back to this camp, let me put this phone up and I'll text you in the a.m. when we get here." "Okay, that's what's up!" said Niecy. And they both hung up. The next day, Jacorius couldn't wait to get to work and get to his phone. He had a couple of fish to fry! Once they got to work, he went straight to his stash spot and grabbed this phone and checked it before he put it on charge. He had a message from Dee-dee {Good morning!} {Good morning!} He was already off of Dee-Dee's thread and was texting Niecy. {Good morning sexy.} She didn't respond to Jacorius right then, at that moment. So he just closes his phone and went outside with the rest of the crew. It was a little after lunch hours, Niecy were texting Jacorius back. {Good morning sexy} Jacorius was sitting in his favorite little cubby hall, in the basement, on the stairs and which lead to an exit door. {Good afternoon sexy} Jacory stood up smiling, looking down in his phone and grabbing his dick at the same time! Obviously thinking about fucking Niecy! Jacorius walked out of the back door, and which led to a couple of alleys. She immediately responded. [Can you talk?} {Yeah.. Give me a sec let me peep the scene.} Jacorius walked down the alley, which led to a road, which had businesses on both sides of the streets.

Then he ran back up the alley, towards the other alley in which led to a parking deck. He peeped the scene and called Niecy. "Hello? What's up with your sexy red?!" "Oh, I'm just chilling, about to get on the road soon." "Oh yeah? What are you going out of town or something?" "No!" laughed Niecy! "That just means that I'm about to get to moving around. So, how long have you been locked up?" I must sound like I'm late as fuck?" asked Jacorius before answering. "Well, I've been gone about 15 years." "15 years?! Wow! Who the fuck did you kill?" Jacorius laughed at Niecy. "Well, he wasn't the president or nothing like that. I had some dope cases also." "Oh a hustler! A dope boy!" "Yeah! Sound like your type?" Answered Jacorius, as he sat the bait for her to bite. "Oh yeah! I can see! Looks like you're getting well taken care of." "Well, I guess you can say that, but I take care of myself mostly. I've been with my husband since I was 17 with four kids! It's a long story I'll tell you about it. What about you? As sexy as you are, I know you got a wife! "A couple of baby mamas and all that! Said Niecy. "No, I don't have a wife. I have one child. A daughter." "Oh okay! Said Niecy. Jacorius and Niecy proceeded to talk for about 10 more minutes. Enough time for him to smoke a joint. "What's that you choking on?" Asked Niecy Some kind of good ass loud! You smoke?" "Yeah! I'm about to fire one up now. I smoke exotic shit! Said Niecy. "You want me to bring you some when I come to class today?" "Hell yeah!" Excitingly answered Jacorius and that's when their relationship started to kick off.

Chapter 4

DECISIONS

After Jacorius got off of the phone with Niecy, him and Malik, was heading back outside, to get back with Johnny and see what the next task was. Upon leaving the staircase coming from the basement to the first floor, they encountered two women heading to the elevator. One was named Maria, and the other one was Latonya, Johnny's nephew's girlfriend. Maria and Malik had something going on! He had been sneaking off and fucking her for months. Maria was a pretty light brown skin, with long multicolor hair, black and brown. She was almost BBW. But she had a very sexy shake with it! She was short about 5'3. Then Latonya was just awesome! Red bone, with an hour-glass shaped body, Stood about 5'5 in, a little past slim thick. Could have been a perfect stripper! Gorgeous face, with some golden and brown eyes, juicy pretty lips, with a small gap in her teeth. She almost look like a young version of sports commentator Lisa Salter. Jacorius really liked her. "Hey ladies, how y'all doing today?!" Said

Malik, as they waited on the elevator. Malik walked over to Maria, to talk and Jacorius almost kept walking till he thought about how fine that Latonya was, so he turned around. Hey Latonya, how you doing today? You working hard?" Said Jacorius, as he approached her. "I'm good! And talking about working hard!? Said Latonya as she rolled her eyes and paused for effect, putting her hands on her hip.

"That's an understatement! They've been slaving us today!" Laughed Latonya. And what about you? You been working hard?" "Hell yeah! That's every day." Said Jacorius. "Them niggaz don't be doing shit!" Said Maria. As the elevator door open. "Yeah! They don't do they don't do they?" Laughed Latonya. "Ride with Johnny and play on the phones." "Well, that's what y'all about to go and do too! Play on them phones!" Laughed Jacorius. "Sho is! About to get in my favorite corner." "Come up there and holler at you sometime?" "Yeah that's cool!" "Okay y'all be easy!" said Jacorius, as they were making their way through the lobby and they seen LaShawn, and Tanethia's aunt Felicia, in the food court. They spoke to them and walked on over to their table. "Hey Lashawn! how you doing?" "I'm fine answered Lashawn. "And you?" "I'm good, about to get back to work." "Okay nice seeing y'all again!" Laughed Lashawn. as she somewhat flirted with Her eyes and Jacorius flirted right back with his! Looking her up and down matching her energy. Malik was talking to Tanethia, another one of his chicks, as Jacorius and Johnny headed down the hall and out the door. "Look like Shawn might be kind of digging you Jay!" Said Johnny. "Shit, I hope she is Johnny, because I'm feeling her like a motherfucker!" "What about that red- bone chic from yesterday?" "Oh you talking about Niecy! I've been on the phone with her this morning! She's supposed to look out for me on something, when she comes to class this evening."

"You already got her toting!" Laughed Johnny, as they were getting into the truck. Malik caught up with them then they pulled off. They rode around the city, to kill some time, while Jacorius and Malik were both on the phone, calling family, friends and their women. "What's up Dee-dee? "What's up with you cuz!" giggled Dee-Dee. Jacorius looked down at his phone and shook his head."Just cooling right now. What you been up to?" "I was just chilling, getting ready for tonight. Got a private show with some Ballin ass niggaz tonight. They are throwing a little birthday party for one of their nephews or something." "Oh word?! Y'all going to get broke off good tonight!" "For sure! Waiting on you to get on out, so you can hit the road with us!" Said Dee-Dee. "I told you, you were going to be our manager!" "I will be out soon! I know you got one of them girls lined up? Said Jacorius, to see where her mind was. "Nigga you don't need one of them. That's bad for business! Shit I'm telling you, just manage and not fuck them. Because if you do, there goes the neighborhood! Jacorius laughed at Dee-Dee. He's already knowing, Dee-Dee wants to be the one to give him some pussy first, out of those strippers Chics.

She's just setting things in place, hoping he rolls with her. After Jacorius got off of the phone with Dee- Dee, he started to stroll through Facebook. He typed in Latonya's name in the search and finally ran up on her profile. He looks through her pictures, and was wondering should he send her a friend request. Jacorius hesitated for a few seconds. Indecisiveness about to go straight out of the window. He pressed the add friend button. That was that! He was going to check her reaction when they go up there later! As they were riding through different neighborhoods, Jacorius Was visualizing the future and the women, who was in his present life now and the possibility of them being in his future. Then, he knows when he gets out, it's a good chance that neither one of those women would be in his future! Because he's served 15 years straight, in prison and was still young and healthy and had an insatiable appetite when it came to women. Decisions! Jacorius called his mother to see how she's doing, and to confide in her about the women in his life and which one he should choose now, and once he get out! "Hey ma! How ya doing?!" "I'm good! How you doing?! "I'm good. Riding around the city chilling. But check it out: I need yo advice on something." "OOH shit! What woman now?" asked Jacorius mother Annette. "I'm trying to make a decision on which one!" "What! What you mean which one?" "I got one, I just met, she married and I have reason to believe she's a dope chic. Looking like money! Another one jugging at me, she's an IT tech.

"Oh, and she married. And.." "Well, I don't want to hear no more, because it doesn't make sense! Married women ain't the way! Get your own woman!" "But Ma, they like me! said Jacorius. "I don't care! Just cause, you say they like you, don't feed off into a situation, that you know is wrong. And then too, you been gone 15 years! You don't really know about being in a relationship for real. So, you might as well just wait till you get out before you just jump in a relationship! And don't just jump into one, time you get out. Play the field. That's my advice Mr!" Said Annette. Jacorius mother. He Couldn't do but laugh. A call was coming through. He looked at his phone, and it was Niecy! How ironic.! "Yo Ma, let me answer this call. This Niecy." "Who is Niecy? Oh that sounds like your dope chic! Okay. Be careful down there!" Said Annette. "Okay Ma, I will!" "Yo! What's up with you?!" "Nothing. I'm down here on campus, sitting in my car. Where you at?" "Oh we headed back that way now. We coming down Jeff Davis. Where bout you parked at?" "In this parking deck behind the bookstore! I'm in a grey charger." "Okay. I know where you at. Be there in a sec." Jacorius Hung up the phone smiling. "Who that Niecy?" asked Johnny.

"Yeah. Johnny you'll pull down in the parking deck behind the bookstore?" "Yeah, I got you!" said Johnny. After a few minutes, Johnny pulled down in the parking deck. Niecy was sitting, camouflaged behind a big truck. Jacorius scanned the parking lot, to make sure that the coast was clear. He got out of the truck and quietly got in the car with Niecy. They both were smiling like chess cats. "What's up Niecy." "What's up!?" Said Niecy, as she slid a tied up sandwich bag, with some loud smelling exotic marijuana in it to Jacorius. He puts it up to his nose to smell it. "Damn! This is smelling good and loud!I Got to get a jar or something." "I got you baby!" Said Niecy, as she reached down in her purse and pulled out a small jar. "This is what I had it in. I didn't think to give it to you, my bad!" "It's cool. But hell yeah, it's going to come in handy. I appreciate you too." "You good! I know how it is. But I got to get ready, to go to class in a few minutes." "Okay what floor is your class on?" Asked Jacorius, Because he was going up on the second floor to get at Latonya! "On the third floor." Answered Niecy, as she was looking at a message in her phone, in which she started frowning at and abruptly closed the text and put her phone down. "Well, I'll meet you on the elevator and ride up with you." "You ain't going to get in trouble?" "Nawl, I can get on the elevator!" laughed Jacorius. "You just go ahead and go to the elevator, by the back door. I'm going to hide this." said Jacorius, as he swiftly exited the charger.

"Yo Johnny, we got anything else to do?" "Nawl, go on and handle your business. We got it." Said Johnny. Jacorius took off down through the alley, in which led to the back door of the basement, where they chilled at, and kept some tools and equipment. He went in the door and down the steps, took a left in which led to a boiler room, type of area. He pulled a loose brick out of the wall and put the jar with the weed in it. He quickly bolted around the corner and up the stairs and out the door. He made it to the elevator, just in time, to catch Niecy, getting on the elevator. Just as the door was closing, Jacorius, stuck his size 12 Timberland boots, in the door, causing them to stop and open back up! Niecy was standing there, In the corner smiling looking somewhat spooked. The doors closed and the elevator started to elevate. "So, can I get a hug or something?" Asked Jacorius. "Sure. You can get the hug, but I don't know about the "something!" Laughed Niecy, as her and Jacorius hugged. "Damn nigga! You all buffed up and shit!" Said Niecy. "Yeah, I work out a little bit."

"Oh, that's why you so sexy?" "No, not really. I was already sexy!" Laughed Jacorius. "I know you smelling good. What that you got on?" "Some Versace Pink." answered Niecy, as the elevator door opens. "Well, this is my destination. I guess I'll talk to you later. You got a phone in the camp?" "No, I leave this motherfucker out here on the job." "Well, can you call me collect? I will accept it." "Okay that's a bet! I will call tonight! When will be a good time?" "Anytime!" said Niecy. "Will do!! See you later sexy!" said Jacorius, as he watched Niecy Walk off. As soon as the elevator closes, Jacorius press two, to go to the admission office, where Latonya worked at. He leaned against the wall in the elevator closed his eyes. "Damn she likes me!" Said Jacorius, thinking about Niecy. The elevator reached the second floor, and the first person he sees heading into the admission office from the back, flaunting and twisting, that curvaceous body of hers, was Latonya! As she turned to go into the admission office, she must have felt Jacorius eyes on her! She quickly looked back at Jacorius watching her ass, with lust in his eyes and she smiled at him, as she crossed the threshold entering the office. "Ummm,uh! Decision" said Jacorius.

Chapter 5

LASHAWN

"Girl, I see the way you and Jacorius was watching each other! Goo- Goo eyeing each other and Thangs!" said Tanethia, as her aunt Felicia and Lashawn laughed. "Girl, ion know what you seen or you think you seen, but that wasn't it!" Laughed Lashawn. Shiiit, I'll be damn!" Said Felicia."Huh?! What am missing? Or should I say what did I miss? Because y'all know something I don't know." Said Lashawn. "Yeah! You missed it, thinking that we missed it! Girl stop!!" Lashawn sat there as if she was discobobalated, looking from Tanithia to Felicia, with her hands up. "Jacorious and I, are only friends! I mean, he's always speaking to me and being nice and I'll be the same towards him! I don't look down on him, because he's locked up. You feel me?" Tanithia and Felicia looked at each other and bursted out laughing. Falling all against each other. LaShawn crossed her arms and just looked at them Shaking her head. "Look Lashawn, I know you don't look down on him. But you do want to look down on him, as he goes down on you! Sucking that spur tongue, with them pussy eating, soup coolers he got!" Said Tanithia. "Whoa! You're the one, who said that you want to ride his dick, why you grip on his big chest!" Said Lashawn. "Tanithia, you said it" screamed Felicia, stopping her laugh, in midair.

"Oh yeah! I did say that!" "So, it looks like, you're the one, with the Googling eyes for Jacorius!" Said Lashawn as she was getting up and preparing to go back to work. She looked at her phone and it was a text from her husband Robert. Just seeing his name made her eyes roll! "Well, I'm about to make my way back to this office." "Okay girl! We'll see you later!" Said Felicia. "Bye girl! I'll see you later!" Said Tanethia. Lashawn was walking down the hall, towards the exit, when she noticed a tall, well-dressed light skin female, long hair, with some heels on. Heading towards the elevator. Then out of nowhere, she sees Jacorius, swiftly get on the elevator with the woman. "Huh! They talking about Jacorius likes me! We like each other! Humph!" She pulls her phone out and texted Felicia. {That dude hoeish and I can tell that he's a thug!} Felicia immediately text back a bunch of laughing emojis. LaShawn text back. {I just seen him following some Redbone on the elevator! lol} {He's just being a man!} Felicia texted back. Lashawn headed on to her office. She sat at her desk, reflecting on things that's going on her life. Her mother's health for one.

She had been going to dialysis, but her health was still somewhat declining. Her daughters were cool. Her career was elevating. But her love life was in shambles! Lashawn and Robert's relationship was on thin ice. She picked her phone up to finally read his text. {Hey baby! I got to go out of town, today on business for the job.} And that was it. She texted him back. {Okay have fun!.} She knew that it was a good chance, that he could be telling the truth, but her woman intuition told her otherwise! That he was lying! Just as she was looking through files and turning her computer on, she receives a text from Robert. {Fun? What do you mean fun?} {Okay Robert! Whatever. Have a nice time!} She texts back and roughly set her phone down. "Hey, easy on the phone!" Said her coworker Reba. A white woman with a bubbly attitude and personality, ironically like Reba McEntire! "Hey Reba! How you doing today?" "I'm fine, just came through to tell you that we have a meeting in 15 minutes." "15 minutes!" repeated Lashawn. "Yep! Mr Conrad called me and told me to tell everyone! Why he didn't email everyone? Beats the shit out of me!" 'Because he's so old-fashioned!" By this time, Lashawn's phone ring and it was Robert! "Hello?" "Why you ain't text me back?" Asked Robert. Lashawn Rolls her eyes to the ceiling before answering and take a deep breath.

"I'm heading to a meeting now and I will talk to you later." Said Lashawn and hung up the phone. Reba looked at Lashawn and took a deep breath. "Come on! Let's go gather up the troops for the meeting." Said Reba, easing the tension in the air. "Yeah, you're right! Let's go rally the troops!" Said Lashawn, as she walked out of her office with Reba. Putting her phone on vibrate, just in case Robert was texting her back.

Chapter 6

3 MONTHS LATER

A few months had done passed and Jacorius had got his freedom! He was out of prison and still working at the college. He had got an old two-door Chevrolet Donk, his cousin had given him. It was sky blue, with a white top and white rally stripes running down the trunk. He had 24-in chrome rims on it. Jacorius and Niecy's relationship was good, while he was in prison, but when he got out, things kind of changed. Niecy was married and still with her husband and they shared a house together, so Jaquarius couldn't move in with her, although she was she was quite ready to move him out and move Jacorius in. But out of respect for her husband and their four children, Jacorius wouldn't let her put him out. Instead, he convinced her to get him a condo. And that's when Jacorius is really put his game in effect! Niecy had money from the dope game! Everyone thought that her husband was the one with the work and money, but all the time it was Niecy! Once Jacorius found out, he started trying to get Niecy to put him on. But she didn't want him to hustle. She wanted him to work, and she would sell the dope. Her game was cocaine! Jacorius didn't really want to sell blow, but he would! Jacorius, being the hustler that he was, he hollered at his play cuz Dee-dee!

He was ready to see, what was cracking in that stripper's world! She had been telling him, that she had wanted him, to be their manager. Help her manage the girls and make a real business out of it. An entertainment management company. She knew he was a pure street nigga, with a lot of hustle and business sense. And to top it off, she wanted to give him some pussy and be a woman in his life! They had been communicating, once he got out. Dee-dee and her strippers came to see Jacorius and Niecy was furious! She had dropped by Jacorius condo, unannounced. They were just sitting around and smoking weed, when Niecy came in. She stood at the door frowning with her hands on her hip. Jacorius stood up and approached her. "Hey baby what's happening?" What's happening!? You need to tell me what's happening!" "Oh, this is my cousin Deedee, I was telling you that was coming down." "Hey, how you are doing baby?" said Dee-Dee, as she stood up to greet Niecy. Niecy reluctantly, shook Dee-Dee's hand. "These are my coworkers." Niecy Barely spoke and walked back to the bedroom.

"Come here Jacorius, I need to holler at you?" Said Niecy. Jacorius looked at Dee-dee, shaking his head as he went to the bedroom. "Yeah, baby what's up?" "Yeah, baby what's up? What them bitches doing in my condo?" Dee-dee my cousin! I told you that. And those are the girls she manage!" "Manage?" "Yeah, manage. And she put me on, by making me be there manager." "Putting you on?! Oh so you're going to manage some strippers? That's what they do right?" "Yeah! Look, you won't help me get on, so I have to figure it out! And now it's figured out! And you got the condo, true enough, but I pay the bills here and the rent!" "Jacorius, I don't give a fuck about none of that! I don't trust your so-called cousin or her little hoes. Look I was going to chill, but fuck this shit! I'm going to leave and when I get back, I want these tricks out of my condo." "Well, we about to hit the road anyway. They got some shows to do,and I'm managing them! That's it! I got shows and parties lined up for them! I'll be gone a couple of days." Said Jacorius, as he walked back in the living room. Niecy stood there stunned! Looking like she just been slapped in the face! She grabbed her purse and stormed out of the condo, slamming the door behind her, as Jacorius texts, the white girl Jan. He was already planning his exit from Niecy. He basically had figured out that Niecy was very jealous and borderline crazy!

Once he got out, his instincts were telling him such, but he kind of overlooked it and storing it in the back of his mind though. Anyway, Jan was over the kitchen, in the cafeteria, at Bethune-Cookman College. Jacorius started talking to her on the low, just as well as he was with the rest of them, he had a thing with. He had fucked her a couple of times before he got out, so now he was going to work her! Jan and her husband had a bar in which they owned among other things. So, she was a lick to Jacorious! After he got through texting Jan, him, Dee-dee and the crew left and hit the road. Jacorius, had it lined up, at a couple of clubs, that his girls were some headliners! They danced, shook their asses, and gave lap dances all night! They visited about three or four clubs that night, so Dee-dee, Jacorius, and the girls had made a nice stack. They went back to a hotel where they rented two suites. One for the girls and the other one was supposedly for Jacorius. They kicked back and smoked and got tipsy, while they counted money. As him and Dee-dee sat there and talked Dee-dee leaned in and grabs Jacorius tool! "Whoa, chill out Dee-dee!" Said Jacorius. Playing hard, trying to keep his dick out of her. A pimp's rule.! "Quit tripping nigga! You know you want it!" Said Dee-dee, as she slammed her mouth on Jacorius shaft. He played hard only for a second and went on ahead and submitted and before he knew it, he was fucking Dee-dee all over the bed! And from that weekend on, he was in the mix!

What made things so sweet, for about 2 months straight, Dee-Dee made sure that her and her three partners was giving Jacorius nearly all of their money they made every night! 5 days a week, to contribute to the cause! On an average, they made 5 to $800 a piece a night. So that was 7 to $10,000 in a week and with the $15,000 he got from Jan, he took off like a rocket! He invested in exotic weed, cocaine, and a bunch of ex pills which he bought through Porsha, his girl from Miami, who knew somebody, who made them, at the University of Miami! He got all of that and flipped it. The job he was working, he had quit. But still went to Henrietta's, every other day. He loved their food... And to see and flirt with the women, trying to catch him one. Specifically, Lashawn. He had done got his mind off of her, temporary that is, till he sees her! And still then, he just kept it friendly and cordial. Held small conversation with her and her friends in passing and kind of kept it moving. He had genuine respect for her, but still with the vibe he sent off, he kept the doors open to possibly get with her! On one particular day, in the parking lot, headed into Henrietta's, Jacorious and LaShawn spoke as usual." Hey Jacorius! I don't see you that much anymore, around the campus, you still work there?"

"No, unfortunately not. But you saw me the other day!" Said Jacorius. "Yeah, but you were standing there with, What's his name? Ernest? And we don't even speak like we used to!" said Lashawn. "I spoke to you then!" laughed Jacorius. "Yeah, I ain't talking about like that! You know you and i used to chit chat said Lashawn. "You're right!" Said Jacorius, as he held the door for Lashawn to walk in. Thinking to himself, "I have been halfway ducking her." "But now Peep this Lashawn: You know one time, you said something to me, almost made me start calling you ma'am!" "Ma'am!?" repeated Lashawn, as they approached her favorite table. Felicia and Tanethia was already there. "Yeah, ma'am! "Laughed Jacorius. "Oh Jacorious, you about to call Lashawn ma'am?" Asked Tanithia, instigating and looking him up and down. "Why were you going to do that?" Laughed Lashawn as she sat down. "Well, a while back I asked you something, and the way you came off on me! I was like damn!" "What you ask me? And when was this?" "It was last year, probably around September, October. I can't remember."

"Last year? Well, you haven't told me, yet what you asked me." "I'll tell you later, when I catch you by yourself." "What?!" Said Lashawn, with a look of surprise. "No! You're going to tell me now!" Yea Jacorius, we want to hear this!" Said Tanethia. "Okay, I asked you for your phone number one day! And you were like, "What? I can get my husband to check up on you!" "So, I was like, no, that's all right. I'll holler at you Later!" "Nooo!" Laughed Felicia, Lashawn, and Tanethia in Unison. "Yeah!" said Jacorius, in a mockingly way, looking at Tanethia. "She probably was on the phone with him." Said Tanethia. "Yeah! That's what it was." Smiled Lashawn, in a flirtatious way. "Oh yeah?" smiled Jacorius. "Uh-huh! I told you Lashawn! Look how he looking at you!" said Tanethia, breaking Jacorius mojo. Him and Lashawn was almost lost in each other's eyes. "Nawl Tanithia." said Jacorius, briefly looking at Tanithia and back to LaShawn, trying to enter her soul! Gazing deeply in her eyes. "She had me, asking her can I take her out for some coffee!" All three women bursted out laughing, cutting the tension in the air. "That thang don't drink no coffee! She drink liquor! You know that!" Said Tanithia. "Yeah he know that! Let me know if you down there or up here now!" said Lashawn, demonstrating with her hand.

Jacorius knew that Lashawn, could have been flirting as usual, but yet he sensed, some serious vibes going on. "Baby I'm turned up, to the maximum! Bucking to the ceiling! What's up?!" Smiles Jacorius, In a swift and cool manner. "Uh huh! Okay?" said Lashawn, rolling her eyes, twisting her lips, into a smile, unconsciously rubbing her hips and rolling her neck, at the same time! In the classical, sassy strong black woman's way. Reflecting the well, seasoned diva, when she want to be. "My God!" Said Jacorius to himself, giving her his best "you turning me on" look. It's a go! "Well look." said Jacorius, as he takes him a seat, smoothly sliding his number to Lashawn. "Hit me up sometimes. Let's talk. I need a lawyer to represent anyway." "Oh, I'm not a lawyer, but if you need one, my friend is." Yet, slyly taking Jacorius number and putting it in her purse. Pausing for a second, Jacorius laughs it off. "Haha, that's cool. Well, I'm about to grab me something to eat, to go. Holler at me sometimes, okay?" "Okay!" Smiles Lashawn. "Y'all ladies take it easy." "You do the same!" replies, Felicia and Tanithia, as Jacorius gets up from the table. "OOO! LaShawn! What's up with that?" Asked Tanithia. "With what?" "Don't Play crazy! You know what I'm talking about, Shawn! Jacorius done slid that number to you!" "Oh my God! Can we discuss something else?" Said Lashawn. "Yeah!" laughs Felicia. Let's do that."

Tanethia leans back in her chair, putting her hand up on her mouth. "Anyway!" said Lashawn, changing and pushing the conversation on, they began chatting about something else. As Jacorius leaves Henrietta's, he's replaying in his mind, what just took place. "Damn, she accepted my number! I wonder if she going to call me. Probably text first." Thinks Jacorius. "I hope she does." Interrupting his thoughts, one of his phone rings. He was operating with three or four now! Jacorius grabbed the phone and checked the caller ID, and it was his street phone. It was some hustlers, out of Alabama He knew. "What's up?" Answered Jacorius. "What it do boy? I'm down on your end, trying to get straight!" It was big baby, out of Alabama. "Okay. Where you at now?" I done hit Daytona Beach!" "Okay give me 10 minutes and I'm coming to you!" "Bet!" Answered Big Baby. Got to get to the money!

Chapter 7

THUG ON HER MIND

"D amn! What am I thinking!? I done accepted this man's number!" Lashawn said to herself, as she rose from the table, getting her purse. "Well girl, let me get on back over here, to the office." "Okay, how your mama been doing?" Asked Felicia. "She all right. She been going through her dialysis and everything, but for the better, overal,l she's okay, thank God! "I know that's right girl! Okay Lashawn, I'm going to sit here 30 more minutes, reading this book, you take it easy, okay?" Said Felicia. "Okay." replied Lashawn, as she headed to the door. Tanethia had already left, 20 minutes ago, as Lashawn and Felicia sat there and politic, about almost everything. Well... Almost everything. Lashawn had purposely, guided the conversation off of Jacorius, so that would give her some time, to really think and soul search by herself. She had a few male friends, but not like Jacorius! She thought that Jacorius, was a good person, cool! But.. He was street! A thug! In which didn't make any difference, but she have never been close to a guy like that. Then a fantasy she had first had when she was 17, went to playing, out in her head, as she got in her car. She was washing clothes in her mother's washroom, which was located in the back of the house! She had on a tube shirt, which was in style, at the time and tight short, short.s She imagined, this guy walking up out of nowhere. By his looks, you can see bad news. "A hoodlum!" Her grandmother used to call them. She wondering, why was he there, approaching her! Looking her up and down. "What you want!?" Lashawn, asked the stranger. "My mother is in the house, up front! Why are you here?" His only response, is him pulling his shirt up, revealing a gun!

"Girl, snap out of it!" said Lashawn, to herself. Bringing herself, back up to date. "What was on my mind back then? Whoa! I got to keep that in control! Whether that was some type of freak fantasy within or some part of her psyche, that yearned, for a street nigga, She had to stay in control! As she drove, the radio didn't make it no better! Mary J Blige, new single was on. "Mr Wrong." Had her thinking hard! Her grandmother's words were in her mind too. "Bad boys always want a good girl, like you to be there woman. They run the streets and put they thing and all them girls they can, but want to have you as they main girl!I" "I feel you Grandma!" Thinks Lashawn, to herself. If she did ever mess around with a thug, he would have to have his stuff together. But must be caring and not crazy! Then she was thinking how Robert has been treating her, as if he didn't care anymore. Like something was going on with him. Like another woman! Actually it was! She walked down on him talking on the phone, one night, telling somebody, "I want you!" Reminiscing, about the look on his face and the excuse he used.

"Hold it, Lashawn! It ain't what you are thinking." "Oh yeah? Well, who is that you talking to?" Not really sure, if Lashawn heard him or not, He said: "look, that was somebody I used to go to school with and she is going through some things! Because she done found out that her husband was gay! and.." "What that got to do with you?" Interrupts Lashawn. "Well... She just needed somebody to talk to,and.. She wants to meet you! I told her about you Lashawn and.." By this time Lashawn had walked off. As she reminisces, about that day, to herself and how faithful she is! All that she gives of herself to people and what she get in return? Nothing! Going through trying times, with her family and every day living. Where is her backbone? Who really has her back? Hard question. It seems like nobody, can be there for her without wanting something in return. "I need to get away! That's what I need to do!" said Lashawn to herself,as she pulled up to the office. As she was getting out of the car, grabbing her purse and phone, she was thinking about texting Jacorius! What harm would it do? They cool with each other. "I give him the 3-day delay. Because Robert, if he don't get right, he's out of here!"

Chapter 8

3 DAYS LATER

Jacorius game had done escalated! The exotic entertainment management company had done grown past local. Thanks to the internet, plugs, family members, and people he just knew from different states. And to add iron to that fire, Dee-Dee and a couple of more girls, up under his management, and got some contracts with Straight Stuntin, Smooth, Black men, and Kings magazine! Keeping his girls booked, to make special appearances at clubs, video shoots or whatever! He was about the loot! The street hustle, he was involved in,X pills, supplier / distributor / wholesaler. Thanks to Porsha, who plugged him in, with some folks, who made them at the University of Miami, he was getting them for the low. 50 cent a pill, because he bought so many, and resold them wholesale for $1.50 a pill to other hustlers, who sold them wholesale! He even used some of the stripper girls, to push them off to other girls when they working. And to other pill hustlers! Playing the middle man.

With the exotic weed, any type of Kush or Purp, he had been going through one of his white childhood friends, who stayed in Vegas, but had a connection in Cali! He always used to say, "If I hustle again, I'm going to be the Plug" He Didn't really sale cocaine, but every now and then, because that invited a new breed of hate.. And danger!Things with him and Jan was kosher.He tried to give her the $15,000 back, she wouldn't take it!

It was game anyway! He was hoping she didn't want it back! Instead, he convinced her to invest in some high-tech stocks. By her being an active day trader and had an account, she plugged Jacorius in and showed him the ropes. He utilized a lot of knowledge he had gained while in prison, so he knew how to keep up with what was going on. Everything was going so good,Jacorius bought him a 2025, drop top XK 150 class Jaguar,from one of Jans friends who owned a dealership in Palm Beach.He moved out of the townhouse Neicy had got.Shit had got so crazy with her! First of all, once he had done really just been out there exposed to so much, now he realizes, he don't really feel her! So one night, he did something he should have been did,he packed his shit and moved out! He had already got a house, through Jan also, in a nice neighborhood. In which nobody knew, where he stayed, except Jan and Deedee. He knew things wasn't going to be on no kind of relationship type of thing, with Dee-Dee, no more than getting money and fucking and she was back and forth to Atlanta anyhow.She wasn't filling the void that Jacorius had, period!While laying back in his bed,just waking up,Jacorius grabbed his phone, And he had a text from a number he didn't recognize."I wonder who this is?" Jacorius.{Hey you! I hope all is well with you.I know you didn't think that I would hit you up. Well surprise smile} "Damn.. It's Lashawn! Ooowee!" said Jacorius. He checked the time that the text was sent. 10:35 a.m. He had just woke up at 11:10 a.m. "Damn! Missed her by 45 minutes. Let me hit her back. Should I call or text? I'll text her back!" said Jacorius.{"What's up? Sorry I missed your text.I was sleeping. What are you up to?"} Not knowing what to expect, as far as how quick she may respond.Jacorius rises out of the bed, to handle the morning things. Shit, shave, and bathe! And try not to be too anxious. Because actually, he was sweating her to hit him back. "She might be at work. Be cool!" said Jacorius to himself, as he commenced to handling his business, turning the shower on.

Chapter 8 (SPLIT)

LASHAWN

"The man might be busy!" Thinking out loud to herself, Lashawn continues to enter data, into her computer. Trying to stay focused on her work, than to continue to think, that it's only been 45 minutes ago, since she texted Jacorius. Just as the thought enters her mind, her phone vibrates and lights up. It's Jacorius! Nonchalantly, Lashawn opens the text and reads it. And smiles to herself. "A mess! Just was thinking about you, but I'm not going to tell him that!" Lashawn lightly giggles to herself. She texts Jacorius back. {What's up to Jacorius? I'm not up to much. Sitting here,at this computer,working. Oh yeah, it's too late to be sleeping, you should be up! Now, what would you be needing a lawyer for?} Not wanting to sound too flirty or inviting, Lashawn tried to keep it business, because he did say something about needing a lawyer, so she thought she would ask him that. 15 minutes at them pass and she set the text to Jacorius and he still hadn't hit back yet! I don't know if he playing games or what things LaShawn. Calm down girl, he might be getting himself together! We just friends anyway. No sweat!

Chapter 8 (SPLIT) (SPLIT)

JACORIUS

As Jacorius was getting out of the shower and drying off, thoughts of Lashawn, hit him at once. Like he was catching some vibes from her! Him being a firm believer in that type of stuff, not superstitious but used to surviving off of his wits! He paid attention to sudden hunches, thoughts, and vibes. So, not trying to seem to anxious, (fooling himself) he quickly got himself together and went straight to his phone to check it. And there it was, a text from Lashawn 20 to 30 minutes ago! "Damn!" Said Jacorius. "No sweat, let me read it."

Smiling to himself, after reading the text, he hit her back. "Had a rough night lol. Oh yeah, about the lawyer, can we speak in person about that? I mean if it's cool! Can you talk now?"

Lashawn

On the phone with Robert, Lashawn was getting agitated, as the text from Jacorius came in! She pulled her phone away from her ear and opened the text and read it, as Robert was yet, kissing up to Lashawn, for being rudely, inconsiderate, uncaring, and absent mind-ed, about things, he should know, concerning his woman! He didn't even know what type of medication, Lashawn had been taking, for the last four and a half years. "Okay Robert, look!" said Lashawn, interrupting him. "I'm going to have to get with you later on this, I got something to catch up on." "Okay then, you going to be like that?" asks Robert. Smacking her lips, Lashawn rushes Robert off of the phone. "Bye Robert!" Hanging up at the same time! "Ooo, I'm getting fed up with him! What got him so, so.. Stupid!" Said Lashawn, knowing but in Denial, that Robert's friend from high school, whom she caught Robert on the phone with, was fucking him silly! "Oh let me answer Jacorius back!" Said Lashawn. After sitting there a couple of minutes, thinking about her and Robert's relationship. {Give me 5 minutes and call me!} Read the text, she sent Jacorius. By now Jacorius, had got fully dressed and was smoking a mini cigarillo of some Irene Kush and was on his other phone, talking business, with some cats out of Georgia. Listening to some Jeezy, as he moved around the house, getting things together. He walked into his room, where his other phone sat on the bed, a text was coming in. He picked the phone up and it was Lashawn. "Call in 5 minutes huh?!" {Bet!}, texts Jacorius, back to Lashawn.

"Okay, bro hit me up when you ready. It's a go!" Said Jacorius, talking to the Georgia Hustlers. Hanging up the phone and reading Lashawn's text again. "Damn! Get a hold of yourself bro! 5 minutes, make it 8 minutes." said Jacorius. Killing a little time, he went on Facebook, checking his inbox. "Oh shit! I keep missing Latonya!" Latonya was a bad Redbone, who worked at the school, in the registration office. He had been holding casual conversation with her, after halfway ignoring her, the time he had been working there. She could tell that, Jacorius wanted her and he could tell that she was digging him. The thing about it, was that she was Johnny's nephew old lady! But now that he didn't work there anymore, he might can go in without any discrepancies. Jacorius had been using this other female, who works in the office with Latonya, to get to Latonya! By going up there, on the fourth floor talking to her, knowing that Latonya would be up there, 90% of the time. So, he had built a dialogue with her, in which had got kind of deep! Deep to the point, that she had inboxes him back one day, telling him out of respect for her relationship, that they should chill out messaging each other... Till now!

What caused that, was one day, she was at the ATM, at the school, Jacorius was walking by and she stopped him in engaged in a brief conversation, saying she haven't seen him in a minute and they flirted a little bit, and he inboxes her, on Facebook, to tell her how good she was looking and now she decides to hit back! {Thanks Jacorius, I try! so how have you been doing?} Jacorius Inboxes her back. {You try?! Are you being modest?. I've been cooling.. What's up with you?} He just had to hit her back! Because Latonya, was a sho-nuff dime piece. Redbone, nice juicy lips, like Pam Oliver, the sports commentator! Almost look like her! About five feet four and made like an hour-glass! With naturally, light brown eyes, like a bobcat! "Damn! Have 8 minutes passed by?" Said Jacorius, as he checked the time. "Yep! Showtime! Let me call LaShawn. Smiling to himself, as he calls Lashawn. After the third ring, Lashawn answers. "Hello?" "Hey, how are you doing?" Asked Jacorius. "Fine!" Giggles Lashawn. "What you doing, sleep this time of day?" "I had went out last night. Rough night!" Laughed Jacorius. "So...What you need a lawyer for?" Asked Lashawn. "Now about that! I wanted to talk to you in person. If it's cool." Now, the wheels are turning in Lashawn's head, always quick on her feet. "Let me check my schedule!" All the time, she is buying time, thinking would that be a good idea.

"Okay!" answered Jacorius. "Don't mean to, interrupt your thoughts, but I can hear the wheels spinning in your head!" laughs Jacorius. "But.. Now I I know you didn't" interrupted Lashawn. "What? Okay my bad!" Uh-Uh! Go ahead and say, what you was about to say." Said Lashawn. "No my bad, I was in error. I'm not rude like that. I apologize." Not knowing, that Lashawn is smiling the whole time! "Umph! That voice." "Excuse me? What you say Lashawn?" "Nawl! Go ahead!" giggles Lashawn. "I was just messing with you. "Okay, what else I was about to say is, well ask, are you having lunch today at Henrietta's?" "Umm, yep. Maybe. "She going to make me chase her!" Said Jacorius to himself, but to the point where Lashawn could hear him! "What you said Jacorius?" "Nothing. Waiting on your answer." "A mess!" Said Lashawn. "Yeah, I'll be there at 1:30." "Okay, that's what's up! I'll be there!" "Okay Jacorius." Okay Lashawn." "Bye-bye." said Lashawn, as she presses the end button, she stares at the phone and smiles. "What this about to be?" Questioning herself. "We just friends." Said Lashawn, as she go back to work, on her computer, but nonchalantly, looks at her watch. "A little over an hour and a half. I'll be there."As Jacorius presses the end button, like Lashawn, he stares at the phone and smiles and sings to his self, "A start of a romance!" "I don't know, but I got to be on point!" Said Jacorius, as he puts the phone down and continues getting himself together and straightening things up in his room, cleaning up and all of a sudden stops!! "I'm feeling.. I'm feeling all floaty and shit!" Looking at his watch."Well, it won't be long now."

Chapter 11

The meeting at Henrieta's

As Lashawn was walking across the parking lot, heading into Henrietta's, she noticed a pretty green convertible pulling in, playing some loud rap music! The car looked foreign. It was hard to tell what kind of car it was. "Dang! That's a pretty car!" said Lashawn. As the car got closer, she recognized the driver. "Is that? Lord have mercy! That's Jacorius!" Jacorius pulls in, customary gangster lean! Arm out the window, flexing a diamond pinky ring and Rolex! Top dropped, Cartier' frames on, looking like a rap star/professional ball player! Flexing! As he got a little closer, she recognized the Jag symbol in the grill. "That's a Jaguar! And a new one at that!" Jacorious noticed Lashawn staring as he was parking. He smiled and waved at her. She smiled and waved back. "I might as well, walk out there and mess with him, about this car!" Thought Lashawn to herself, as she turned around and headed to the parking lot. "Hey you!" Said Lashawn, as she walked up to Jacorius, as he was letting the top up on the car.

"What's up Lashawn?!" smiles Jacorius. "You Looking good today! As everyday!" "Well thank you! Look... What is this, a transformer car or something? This thing is beautiful!" "Thanks! This is a Jag SK8." Said Jacorius.

"I know! I see that symbol in the grill." said Lashawn. As she walked around the car, touching it in spots. "What kind of green is this, a metallic?" Emerald. Candy coated!" Answers Jacorius. "Okay! Then you done put some rims on it!" Said LaShawn, as she stopped in her tracks, looking at Jacorius, disapprovingly. "What?" Asked Jacorius,Admiring Lashawn's girly demeanor. "You know you don't supposed to put no rims on no car like this!" "I feel you! But we only live once! Check this out. Let's go on, to catch us a table and politic. Your crew aint here today?" Asks Jacorius, as him and Lashawn proceeded to walk towards the entry of Henrietta's. "No! I don't think they coming today. I don't know. I haven't talked to any of them." Jacorius and Lashawn, sat down at her favorite table and ordered something to eat. They sat there and chit chatted, as they waited on their order. "So you haven't told me, what you needed a lawyer for yet?" "Oh yeah!" Said Jacorius. "Okay. You know I done been to Prison...Right?" "Right." Answered Lashawn. "I'm trying to get this sentence off of me." "Okay. I'm not following you. What are you trying to do, get a pardon or something?" "Well. Yeah. But actually, I need some post-conviction relief." "Post conviction relief?" "Yea!" said Jacorius.

"Well, you need to tell me everything, from beginning to the end." "About me or about my cases?" Lashawn looked at Jacorius, twisting her lips, like "you know what I'm saying." "What?" Laughed Jacorius. He knew, she was talking about his cases, but also, he knew, she was taking a step, to really get to know him. "Look... You want me, to give you my friends number, so you can talk to her? If you don't trust me?" Jacorius laughed and looked Lashawn in the eyes, a couple of seconds, before answering. "No. I trust you!" "I feel special!" Said Lashawn, smiling."You are. You're an angel!" "Huh!? Not quite. I just do what's good from the heart. You know help someone if I can, if they're good people. And Jacorius, I've been told You, I think you are a good person."That's rights!" said Jacorius."Number nine, and order number 10." Yelled a young Puerto Rican waitress. "That be us!" Said Jacorius, signaling, the waitress over to their table. "Hey Miss Lashawn! How are you doing today?" asked the waitress. "Hey Anita girl! You working hard?" "A little. Miss Lashawn, when you have time, I need to talk to you about something." Anita, what I told you about that miss stuff?" Playfully fusses Lashawn. "Oh my bad!" laughs Anita. "You're okay Nita. I catch up with you later okay?" "Okay Lashawn!" laughs Anita. Actually, Lashawn was trying to cut Anita off, because she didn't want Jacorius, to know that she owned Henrietta's!

As Jacorius and Lashawn ate, they discussed Jacorius situation, and she wants to know everything! Details and all! He kind of felt uncomfortable, telling Lashawn about the murder case, he did time on, even though they've always been friends. When he got to the part, of the actual death blow, he kind of spared her the actual details. "Seem like you ain't telling me everything! But I get the picture." Jacorius kind of laughed her at her boldness off, but at the same time admired it. "Okay. Now, tell me about the drugs." "Okay." said Jacorius and he started telling her, about how he got the drug case. Even though, him telling her all this didn't really matter, he just went along with the charade! "Now, how are you going to relate, all this to your home girl? You got a good memory?" Lashawn Giggles, as she held up the recorder. "I told you! You were slick!" Said Jacorius. He already had noticed the little device, shaped like an ink pen, when she first got it out of her purse, along with her phone. "Slick?" Asked Lashawn. "Not hardly." They commenced to laugh and talk as they ate. "So, what are you doing nowadays, since you're not working at the school anymore? You must've found a better job? Going by what you're driving." Said Lashawn."

Well, actually I got my own business now." Said Jacorius. "Oh yeah? What kind of business you got?" "Exotic entertainment management." "What!?" screamed Lashawn. "Whoa, Whoa! Calm down Ms. lady!" laughed Jacorius, as he leaned forward, motioning with his hands, playfully. "Now.. Hold up! Soo, enlighten me. Who you manage? Strippers and stuff?" "Yeah. Why are you acting so surprised?" Lashawn slowly leans back in her chair, and she studies Jacorius. "A pimp!" Said Lashawn. "No!" Laughed Jacorius. "Yes it is Jacorius! It's just legalized. Because, you know some of them girls, will end up selling they goods, for money and you probably get all them girls money!" Actually, Lashawn was right, to a certain degree. Because he did have a call girl / dating service, under his exotic management umbrella. But he wasn't taking all of their money, nor into any '70s/80s pimp type of shit. Gorilla pimping, you know kicking his hoes ass and all that. If you wanted to match it to Pimpin, it would be more of a finesse thing. Operating off of some game, his cousin Sonny from Orlando, who was really pimping in the late '70s and early '80s. And that is, "Use your tools! If you got the tools to draw women, charm and charisma, use it wisely. Use it to get what you want out of her! And that is money! Keep that dick out of her, cause that's what all of them, you would have, would be competing for! And that is to be your bottom broad, your main lady!" Jacorius explained to Lashawn, how he was putting it down. "So.... Them women, I seen you with, that night at the comedy club, they work for you?"

"Under my management." "Same thing!" Said Lashawn, rolling her eyes. One of Jacorius phone was going off. He had two with him! This was the one on him not the one on the table, which was visible. It had been getting texts and a few phone calls, while they talked and ate. He answered this one though. "What's up?" It was some hustlers from Jacksonville, down to spend some money with him. "Okay, get back with me in 10 minutes." Lashawn, being curious but careful, smiled and said "Hope I'm not out of place! But who was that, you talking about meeting in 10 minutes? Leaving me here, by myself!" Lashawn question was cute. "I was just playing with you, it ain't my business." "No you cool. It's business though." Said Jacorius, as he got it from the table. "Check this out, we'll continue this conversation, maybe later, perhaps tonight?" Asks Jacorius. As Lashawn smiles, playfully and unconsciously twirls a strand of her hair! She gives Jacorius question a little thought.. "Maybe." "Text, call, or what?" Asked Jacorius. "Text first. We'll see." Said Jacorius. "Okay Lashawn" said Jacorius, as he pushes his chair in. "I'll hit you up later, you have a nice day, okay?" "You do the same Jacorius." Smiled Lashawn. She picks up her phone, like she was checking it, but actually she was using that move, as a decoy! An attention deflector, because she was halfway blushing like a teenager with a crush and with the other customers in the cafe, the nosy ones, probably was watching! Lashawn watched Jacorius, as he swaggered out of the door. That's another reason she grabbed her phone, she didn't want him to know that, she was actually into him... A little bit. As he walked outside, she noticed Jacorius and this young girl, around the age of 21-22 speak to each other.. Smiling! But Jacorius didn't stop to talk to her, but she noticed the way the young lady blushed and slightly looked back at Jacorius. Something he might have missed! But something women don't miss from other women. "Snap out of it girl! It's nothing. Then he's not yours anyway."

Thought Lashawn to herself, as she still casually sized her possible competition up.

Her and Jacorius had talked earlier that day, and, in the past, she noticed while talking to her, Tanethia, and Felicia, a lot of women looked at them. Him, then to her. She would playfully ask Jacorius: "Do you know her? or "Y'all used to talk? or still talk?" And at times, how Jacorius would be wondering and saying, "Who is that lady, looking all down through here?" And Lashawn, would tell him: "Maybe she wants to get with you!" Most of the times, Jacorius would deny it or say: "I can't tell! She haven't made a move. And Lashawn would tell him that, maybe she's waiting on the right time to make a move. "Or maybe she's waiting on you!" I'm a woman, I know! And he would laugh it off. "Jacorius and all of his women!" said Lashawn to herself as she sat there and evaluated the situation, her situation. Then Jacorius is a hustler! "He ain't fooling me!" said Lashawn. A thug! I can't get involved with nobody like that! A street man! Especially with the job I got!" Then at the same time, in her heart, she always wanted a street nigga! A strong man! With some sense! And it wouldn't hurt, if he was a drug dealer! Even though, she's always done for herself, like she was raised to do, but every woman wanted to be spoiled, every now and then.

All of a sudden, from somewhere in her psyche, that reoccurring fantasy came to surface! Same guy, same washroom in the back of her parents' house, when she was 17 or 18. "I told you my mother was up in the front of the house! Before she knew it, the thug had his hands around her butt and in kind of a rough way, he pulls Lashawn up on his hard dick and pausing for a brief moment. Looking her in her eyes and kissing her slow and deep! With her only putting up, a slight resistance before, returning the kisses just as deep! Hard and passionate, moaning as they kissed and her moans was exciting this thug, making him pick her up and put her on the washing machine. He pulled her tube shirt, over her head, exposing her breasts and started sucking them in a hungrily way! "Lashawn. Lashawn!" Said Anita The waitress, snapping Lashawn out of her fantasy, from when she was a teenager. "Oh! My bad!" laughs Lashawn. "I had done left here for a minute." "I know! Are you okay?" "Yeah, yeah, girl. Just some old stuff on my mind. So what's up with you Anita? What you want to talk about?" Actually Lashawn was glad that Anita interrupted her. "What done came over me?" said Lashawn to herself. Anita was telling Lashawn about her problem, she was having at the cafe with co-workers and as well problems at home. As the owner of Henrietta's, Lashawn had always established, with her employees, management on down, to talk to her about anything!

She is just that type of person. Never meets a stranger. But careful, not just let anybody get close to her, or get in her inner circle. Friendly, but not Mary Poppins friendly! To some of her staff at the cafe, she wears the mother hat but can switch to the best friend and the auntie, you can go to, as your confidant. After talking to Anita, she went and checked on a couple of more people who worked there and a couple of customers. She laughed and chit chatted with and hugged a few. She was touchy feely like that. After Lashawn made her presence felt and said goodbye to almost everybody, she headed for her car, checking her phone. She had a text from Robert! Things were on Rocky Ground with him, right now, but nevertheless, she opened and read his text. {Where are you?} Read the text. "Now.. Here you go with these silly questions! [The usual. At this time of day!] Answered Lashawn. [Oh. Just checking.] texted Robert. Standing at her car, about to text Robert back, Lashawn changes her mind, puts her phone in her purse and jumps in her car, cranks up and pulls off and heads back to work.

As she was in traffic, Lashawn was thinking about her and Robert's relationship, and how it was crumbling. How he had been acting, like he didn't care. Pulling dumb moves, like he was actually trying to see where Lashawn was, so he can time her in order for him to play! Because he knew that Lashawn Stayed busy. Actually, besides her liking to be involved in school activities, where both of her daughters, used to attend, she actually was doing a lot of things like that, to kind of deal with her problems with Robert and her family. Since he wasn't big on help these days! As she was riding, one of Mary J Blige songs came on the radio. "Mr Wrong." And immediately her mind went into overdrive! Thinking about Jacorius. "Bad boys ain't no good! Good boys ain't no fun!" Now, this was so N-Sync with what was going on with her, that she almost got chill bumps! Because, with Jacorius, he had this bad boy image, in which deep in her mind, she was attracted to! "Maybe, that's why I've been having that same crazy fantasy since a teenager." Thought Lashawn to herself. Evaluating the situation in her mind, she came up with the notion, that Jacorius was a good person, whom a curveball, has been thrown to in life! Just playing the cards in which was dealt to him. He's not crazy! He is a thug, but he is about his business. Even though, she didn't like the business he was involved in! And whatever else he might be involved in. She knew he was a lady's man, a player! How he treats his woman and everything else that counts in a relationship with her, she don't know if he's capable of handling. That is yet to be seen!

Chapter 12

Start of a Romance

Jacorius, being the workout enthusiast he is, trying to keep his physique up, was at the gym working out. He got an inbox, through messenger, from Latonya. "Damn!" Said Jacorius. "Got to see, what this baby talking about." He Finished a set of butterflies, before reading the message. Jacorius opened the message. [Hey Jacorius! How have you been doing? Would have been got back at you... Been busy. you understand! And no, I'm not being modest. Like I said. I try!] Jacorius sat there baffled, trying to figure out, what Latonya was talking about. So, he went back through his sent messages, to see what he said to her, because it had been a couple of days or better, since he sent her a message. "Oh! Now I see!" Jacorius had told her, that She was looking good and asked her was she being modest, when she replied, "I try" from the last message. "I'm going, to her office, at the school." Said Jacorius. [Okay! if it's no problem, I will be over there, to pay you a short visit! Cool?] Jacorius sent his reply, back to Latonya.

As he was waiting on her answer, Lashawn was on his mind, at the same time! "Damn! I'm in a hell of a position!" Said Jacorius. He was thinking like that because, he still had a void he wanted and needed to fill. Since, the unofficial breakup, with Neecy, he really wasn't just looking for a main woman to call his own. He was now definitely, into just fucking! Having cut friends. Besides, it seems he have always drawn other people women to him! Married or in a deep relationship.

That didn't really matter to him, because he only caught feelings for Neecy. But the rest of them, He wasn't falling in love with. Besides, fucking other dudes' women, so easily, made him shy away from relationships, but at the same time, he still had that void to fill. He wanted his own! And Latonya and Lashawn, was his ideal women to make his own. He was kind of stuck between the two! He felt like he knew Lashawn better and it was something about her, besides her body and cute face. Latonya was younger, super fine! Eye candy magazine action! Jacorius was getting to know her. She had let it be known that she wouldn't be second behind no woman! Actually, Jacorius wanted to Fuck Latonya bad! Yeah Lashawn, he wanted to fuck her also, but he wanted her as wifey! Jacorius phone vibrated. A message from Facebook, kind of confirmed his thoughts. It was from Latonya! [Yea Jacorius! It's cool for you, to come to the office. If you can, could you come now? Where are you?] Jacorius hit her back, ASAP! [Okay. I'm at the gym, but I'm on my way!] Jacorius grabbed his phone and gym bag and headed out the door! Once he got in the car, for some strange reason, he texts Lashawn! She was on his mind heavy. [Hey Lashawn! How are you today? Hope you're not working hard.] After he hit the send button, Jacorius crunk up the Jag and pulled off.

Lashawn was sitting at her desk, stressing when Jacorius text came through. Funny, because at the time, he had been vaguely on her mind! Lashawn opened the text and read it. Now Lashawn was thinking, should she put her mask on and put up a front like everything was cool or should she keep it real with Jacorius and let him know that, actually she was stressing! She felt comfortable enough, with Jacorius, to let him at least know, that she was stressing. "Yeah, I'll keep it real with him, to see how he responds" said Lashawn to herself. {Hey Jacorius! No, I'm not working hard, never that! I'm stressing a lil bit today... but I'm okay. What you up to?} After Lashawn sent the message, she sat her phone down, took her glasses off and closed her eyes and began massaging the top of her eyes. Thinking of her latest episodes. First it was Robert: all of the things she thought he was, he turned out not to be! She's not so sure, about there engagement, there wedding, there relationship and all! Then next, the episodes with her family. Mother, sister, and brother. She was thinking, if only Daddy was here. Her mother, was going through her dialysis treatment, but other health problems existed. She had a couple of mini strokes, the year before and that had Lashawn kind of worried, because her brother and sister was living at the house with their mother and at times, they got on their mother's nerve. Lashawn would ask her mother, "Why do you put up with things, you put up with? Or why do you help them grow folks so much mama? You never help me like that." And her mother's reply, mostly would be: "Well Lashawn, you're stronger than them." Lashawn was at her wits end, trying to figure all this out. She had been talking to her god brother, twin about things, and a few more of her friends, but it wasn't nothing like the comfort of a companion. "I need a vacation and just get away from everybody!" said Lashawn. Lashawn grabbed her phone, to see had Jacorius text her back yet. "Nope! I wonder where he's up to?"

Headed to the college, to go see Latonya, Jacorius was on the phone, with his daughter Jasmine, who stayed up in Jacksonville. When a text came through. Normally Jacorius would ignore texts, when he's on the phone, but he couldn't keep his mind off of Lashawn, so he just had to check it. "Hold on Jazz." "Okay?" He opened the text, and it was from Lashawn. "Damn, I wonder what's up with her. She's stressing." "Who you talking about pops, one of your girlfriends?" asked Jasmine. "What I tell you about that pop stuff. Said Jacorius. Jasmine started laughing. "Well, you are a pop!" "Okay, you must don't want me to go to the car lot for you?" laughed Jacorius. "Yeah, I'm just saying. Dad."

said Jasmine, being sarcastic. "Well, check this out jazz, I'm about to walk up in this school, I'll get back at you in a minute." "All right. Bye." said Jasmine. Jacorius pulled into the parking lot, of Bethune, Cookman College. Found a parking spot, parked and immediately texts Lashawn back. [I'm just cooling Lashawn, glad to hear from you! I'm just leaving the gym and about to walk up in the school for a minute. For what is worth, try not to stress too much, and oh yeah, if it's cool, we can talk. I'm a great listener!] Jacorius sent the message to Lashawn and walked up in the college, to the elevator, and to the fourth floor, to the register's office. To see what's popping with Latonya!

Lashawn received the text and read it with a smile on her face. [So, you're great listener huh? Call me when you get a chance, we can talk.] She sent the message and sat back. Jacorius was in the registration office, talking to Latonya when the text came through from Lashawn. In a kind of subtle manner, he opened the text and read it, looked at the time and decided that he would kick it there for 30 minutes and he would call Lashawn. Got to get to her! Jacorius and Latonya talked and flirted with each other. Both trying to calculate, each other's move! So, Jacorius, decided to go ahead and crack her! "Check this out: When can I take you out?" Latonya acted kind of shocked. Yet she was smiling. "Well, I don't know about that right now. You know I'm involved with someone right?" "Umm, Yeah!" said Jacorius. "Oh, it don't matter to you huh?" said Latonya. "No, not really." Jacorius and Latonya sparred back and forth, until she decided that she'll think about it. "Can we talk tonight, when you get off?" "Yeah, text me first." "Okay, but check this out." said Jacorius, looking at this watch. "I'm about to bounce, I'll get at you later, okay?" "Okay you be easy." "Bet!" Heading to the elevators, Jacorius immediately speed dials Lashawn. Even though, he was up there on the 4th floor, trying to connect with

Latonya, to see what's really going on with her, his mind was racing back to Lashawn.

When Jacorius's call came through, she was walking through the doors, of Henrietta's, smiling looking at the caller ID. "It's Jacorius" said Lashawn. "Hello?" Hey how you doing? Asked Jacorius. "Hey! How are you doing?" "Just cooling..Now how are you feeling?" Lashawn letting out an exhausted sigh for effect, as she sat her purse down, at her favorite table and paused before answering. "I'm.... I'm okay." "Come on with it now! Talk to me. I told you I'm a great listener." Said Jacorius, gently urging Lashawn on. "I know, I know. It's just so much! Well first and foremost, issues dealing with my family." Lashawn was briefly filling Jacorius in, on what was going on with her and what had her stressing. "Look, where are you now?" Asks Jacorius. "I'm at Henrietta's." "Damn...That's a coincidence. I was headed that way!" "Oh, okay! I'm here." Giggles Lashawn. "I will be there in 5 minutes! I'm on the freeway right now." "Okay. Okay! I'll holler at you then!" said Lashawn, as she hung the phone up. She was thinking to herself, Jacorius seem to be a caring man! "Well I have to see about that! See what his main motives are. I know he wants me, but is it genuine?" All these thoughts were going through her head, when Jacorius walked through the door, dressed like a college football player, coming from an NFL combine! The tryout session, for the NFL.

He was dressed in a tight black, Under Armor shirt, black baggy shorts. Some black Nike Air Max tennis shoes, black footies. "Oh my God! What is he trying to do to me? Where are you coming from? The gym?" "Not exactly. I was there earlier, when I text you. What? I stank or something?" Asks Jacorius. "Nawl!" laughed Lashawn. "I was just looking at what you got on. Looking Jacorius up and down. Jacorius smiles. "Oh this tight ass shirt? I know you ain't used to seeing me where nothing like this! This my, "Um Flexing Shawty" shirt!" "What?? a mess!" said Lashawn. Jacorius pulled a chair out and took him a seat. With a semi-serious look in his eyes and asks Lashawn: "Now. What's really going on with you? Are you okay?" Jacorius, not knowing, but this just about melted Lashawn! His genuine concern for her. She sat her favorite clear green cup down, paused for a second or two and proceeded to tell Jacorius, what was going on with her. He listens to her intensely. Eye contact on point. Nodding to show her, he was really paying attention and subtly prodding her on, with the small comments like, "oh yeah?", Etc. in agreement with her, when it's appropriate. Just being a good listener and not judgmental. Jacorius and Lashawn had sat there at Henrietta's, for at least 2 hours! Bonding, not even paying attention to the time. They were so into each other, they barely paid attention to their surroundings, until this young college female, the same Redbone with long curly hair, Lashawn noticed, the other day, speaking to Jacorius. Rather they spoke to each other, when he was leaving, and she sits in the same spot every day! Near Lashawn. "Hey!" spoke the young red bone. Lashawn looked up and spoke at the same time. "Hey what's up?" said Jacorius. "You talk to her or something?" asks Lashawn. "Nawl!" laughs Jacorius. "Why you ask me that?" "The way she was looking! Then. Matter of fact, the way, all of a sudden, she be watching me!"

"Noo"! laughs Jacorius. "Yeah! Uhh huh!" laughed Lashawn, Shaking her head. "I think she likes you." "Don't do that Lashawn! Why you always do that?" "Do what?" "Putting all these women on me!" "Because! I'm a woman! I might see stuff you don't!" Well, look you might be right, but I already got my sights set on someone." Said Jacorius. As he leans on the table, both elbows, rubbing his hands, in a conspiring manner. "Oh yeah?" asks Lashawn. "Yeah!" answered Jacorius. Looking down with a smile on her face, slowly shaking the ice up in her cup. "Well, who might that be?" "You of course!" "Oh yeah?!" "Yeah!" Said Jacorius, mocking Lashawn. Lashawn Giggles, being her always cheerful self. "A mess!" Said Lashawn. "Well, I'm kind of in a situation. But we'll see". "Okay! No pressure." said Jacorius. At that time, that's when Jacorius phone vibrated. Actually, it had been vibrating off and on, the whole time he was talking to Lashawn! But he wanted some, almost quality time with her. He looked at the caller ID and it was the usual. Some money! "Let me take this call. Okay?" "Okay, go ahead." said Lashawn as Jacorius answers the phone, Lashawn grabbed her phone, checking messages as well.

Her mind was in overtime, thinking about everything! "Check this out Lashawn, I apologize, but I got to run! Can we talk later on tonight?" "Yeah, that would be cool!" 'Okay, I'll call you! And you have a nice day." "You do the same Jacorius. As Jacorius was leaving Henrietta's, she sat there, thinking to herself, why didn't she tell Jacorius, that she was engaged to be married, in the next five or six months?! Deep down in her heart, she knew why she didn't tell him. Things between her and Robert wasn't what you would call kosher and besides, she really likes Jacorius! "I'll just have to see how things flow." Said Lashawn to herself. As Jacorius is riding to go and make this money, his mind was still on Lashawn. Hard! Even though Jacorius has plenty of women, not to mention Latonya was on deck, ready! But it was something about Lashawn, had him wanting to really pursue a real relationship! Oh boy!

Chapter 13

CHOOSING BETWEEN 2 WOMEN

That night, Jacorius talked to Latonya and Lashawn. But he actually rode out on the phone, seriously with Lashawn! Latonya, she has great conversation and to top it off, he wanted to fuck her badly! She is eye candy, No question, hands down! The average man would love to have her as his old lady, boo thang, main squeeze, whatever! Lashawn, she has great conversation, very down to earth. Looks great! Fine, but what she had on Latonya was experience and it was just that something about her, which took the lead in Jacorius mind. Wifey material! A woman! Latonya was a woman also, but it was just that, something about Lashawn. One thing Jacorius learned, over the next following weeks, from communicating with Lashawn, was that they were in sync with each other. That was part of that something, that he couldn't put his finger on! And she agrees with him on that. To put the icing on the cake, Jacorius really listens to her. Never judging her, never putting a rush on her, about sex or a relationship. Just letting things flow, like she wanted it.

At first, neither party wanted to admit, that they had growing anxiousness, or should we call it anticipation? When Lashawn is at work, she be anticipating Jacorius calls or texts, because he would wait for her to get to work and get settled in and text her a good morning, how you are feeling, how did you sleep. etc. Didn't matter what he was doing, that was a ritual. Then his anticipation, was in response from Lashawn. He would text her in the morning, if she wouldn't hit right back or at least an hour later, he would get kind of antsy. He knew that she probably would be busy at times, so he will understand her tardiness, but the fact remains the same, he was sweating a response! Careful not to be pushy, Jacorius finally broke the silence, about the matter and funny, Lashawn was on the same page as Jacorius. "I don't mean any harm asking you this Lashawn, but...What be taking you so long, to get back at me?" Asks Jacorius, laughing. "I ain't going to tell you no lie, but I was going to ask you the same thing!" Said Lashawn Giggling. "You serious?" "Yeah, I'm serious! Especially when you be making me sweat! At least that what it seems like." said Lashawn. "Because I be doing something, then I get your text and I'll be like, oh let me hurry up and get back to you."

"Oh, you be making me sweat? I knew it!" laughed Jacorius. "No, you be making me sweat! Because I know you can text me earlier than what you do. You be up!" Said Lashawn. Actually, at times Jacorius will make her sweat, because he was thinking that maybe, she was making him sweat, and he didn't want to seem too needy! But all the time, he was Lashawns' therapy, to a certain degree. And she be wanting him to contact her. "Well check this out Lashawn, I do be up early, most of the times and sometimes, I just be getting in." "Oh, I forgot! You be out pimping them girls, who dancing for you! And Whatever else you be up to!" Said Lashawn. Jacorius blurted out laughing. "No, what I told you about that?" "It's the same thing! No matter how you try to dress it up!" Said Lashawn. "Okay. Back to the matter at hand." Said Jacorius I'll make sure to text you a little earlier. Is that cool?" "Yeah... That's cool!" "And oh yeah, Here's my work number also. Call that number, most of the time, if I'm at my desk." "Okay I'm going to lock it in. "Oh yeah! "When are you going, to let me take you out or something? Or maybe you can come through here!" "Let me think about that. I haven't built my nerves all the way up for that yet!" said Lashawn. "Okay that's cool." Said Jacorius. "That's what I'm talking about!" Said Lashawn. "What you talking about?" asks Jacorius.

"See, I'm going to, go on and tell you. You're my Kryptonite!" "Your Kryptonite?" Laughs Jacorius. "Yeah! I'm trying to stay strong and do the right thing you know? About my situation." "Yeah, I know." answered Jacorius. "See, with the average guy, I can turn them down and they'll keep on trying and I feel no weakness towards them! With you, when I turn you down, you just be like: "okay cool." "I feel where you are coming from, but I can only do what you allow me to do!" "That's what I'm saying! I just might allow you to have your way! Why you think I haven't been done went somewhere with you? I don't play with fire!" Said Lashawn. "Oh. So, I'm fire? Asks Jacorius. "Yeah! To me." Jacorius and Lashawn got quiet. Then he lets out a slow, seductive laugh. "Okay. You know I'll never pressure you. Right?" "I know." said Lashawn. From previous conversation, Lashawn had let it be known, that she wanted to be kept, by a caring, loving man. And that she wasn't a temporary type of girl. She let that be known, quick one day that she wasn't temporary. She had mistaken Jacorius for just wanting to briefly, just comfort her for a moment. Wanting to just get a quickie or something. She was stressing that particular day, so he had asked her to come over for a minute, to possibly work it out, and she was like; "Do I come off as being temporary? A temporary girl." He's straightened it up; by letting her know, He didn't take her as being temporary and he got the picture and told her he was just trying to give her a little comfort.

It was strange for Jacorius, being the type of man, he was, to not to just straight dismissed Lashawn and be on to the next one. "If we ain't freaking, we ain't speaking" type of thing. Or how can she contribute to the cause? His cause! But with Lashawn, he recognized that she is a woman who he genuinely cared about. A woman who was really going through some trying times. So, Jacorius was letting her know, that he truly was caring and didn't want nothing from her. Just want to be there to hold her. In turn, he is so caring that he makes her body ache and yearn for him! But he wants to prove that he is deeper than just sex and he is the one holding strong. Jacorius could tell that Lashaun's man/situation wasn't handling his business anymore, and that he really didn't care to much about her anymore. From the things that Lashawn would tell Jacorius about her and Robert's relationship and he could tell that Robert was tired of her! The relationship and did things like he didn't give a fuck. Jacorius wouldn't never pour salt on dude, or voice his opinion about dude, but by Jacorius being a man, he knew what was up! He just didn't tell her. "Oh, by the way Jacorius, did I tell you that I was high maintenance?" Said Lashawn. "Hi maintenance?!!" repeated Jacorius. "You don't come off as being high maintenance to me." "Yes, I am! Probably not in the sense you're thinking. I'm spoiled! I want what I want, when I want it!" Said Lashawn. "Oh. Okay, I got you!" Said Jacorius. "Oh, you got me?" Asks Lashawn. "Fa sho!" said Jacorius. They conversated a little longer, till Lashawn got a little busy at work and they agreed to talk a little later. "I want you to give me about an hour and make sure you call me back. Text me and I'll let you know whether or not to call my desk. "Okay." said Jacorius.

After they hung up, Jacorius rolled a blunt, of some Irene Kush and sat there thinking about the whole situation. "Damn, she is feeling me like I'm feeling her! "Will I make her my old lady or what?" Right when that thought hit him, his phone rings and it was Latonya! "Hey, what's up Latonya! How are you doing?" 'I'm just cooling, what's up with you?" "Nothing. Trying not to let these folks get on my nerves today!" "Okay." "You remember when I told you, I would think about letting you take me out?" "Yeah... Of course I remember. "Well... I thought about it, and I decided that, I'm going to let you take me out!" "Okay! That's what's up!" Said Jacorius. "But under one condition." Said Latonya. "Okay, what's that?" That we leave Daytona Beach." "Oh! So, what's going on? You and your old man have problems or what? Y'all still together? Talk to me!" "Well... We've been having problems, that's nothing new. We on the verge of breaking up! Seriously! You remember a while back, when you asked me was I happy and I told you that I was content, in my situation, till God see fit? Until something better comes along?" "Yeah... I do." said Jacorius. "Well, that's where I'm at right now. Maybe something better has come along." Said Latonya.

"Okay! I see where you're coming from." Said Jacorius. His mind was in full overdrive now! He wanted to fuck Latonya badly! But making her his main girl, the future was kind of dim for that. Lashawn had definitely moved in, as a great possibility on that turf. But at the same time, Lashawn hadn't just committed fully, to being Jacorius girlfriend and Robert's ex! Besides, he's still fucking other women, what would one more hurt? Knowing damn well, that Latonya wasn't going for being girlfriend number two! "Fuck it!" Jacorius said to himself. "I will fuck with Latonya on the low and hope she don't get too serious and wait to see what Lashawn was going to do. "So, when do you want to go out?" "Umm, tomorrow night is cool! By it being Friday. That's if you're cool with it." "Yeah! I'm cool with it. So, what time should I pick you up?" "Around 7:00." "Okay! Where do you want to go?" Asks Jacorius. "It doesn't matter! Well, as long as it isn't one of those wild clubs, where a bunch of youngsters at... And oh yeah, to be on the safe side, let it be out of Daytona Beach. You understand!" "Yeah, I do!" laughs Jacorius.

"I don't have to worry about no drama, do I?" "No... You don't. I mean, me and Tywan is on bad terms and like I said, it's about to be over with. "Okay now Latonya, I hear you... You know I don't need no trouble! You know my situation! "I know!" Said Latonya. He isn't that crazy, but I don't feel like arguing with him. And I just want to get away for a little bit! You don't have to worry about it!' Jacorius wasn't worried about it, because even though he's an ex-felon. He stayed strapped! He just didn't want to be put in a do or die situation...Over a woman! " "Okay, it's on! Said Jacorius. "I'll see you tomorrow!" Said Latonya in a soft seductive way. "Yeah... Okay Latonya. Said Jacorius. They exchanged their goodbyes and hung up. "Damn!" Said Jacorius. "What the fuck am I going to do?!" Well, it wasn't no secret in what he was going to do. He was going to fuck Latonya, Point Blank! Now he was sitting there, thinking where he would take her. Then Lashawn bombarded his consciousness. He was thinking and wishing he could be taking her out! Well, in due time it'll happen. Anything takes long will last long! "I'll take my time with her." Said Jacorius to himself. "Choice has been almost finalized but let me fry this other fish, while I got her on the hook! Play on player!"

Chapter 14

FRIDAY

"Hey look here, I ain't going to be able to mob with y'all tonight. I got something to do, so Dee-dee gather everybody up, so y'all will be on time for your flight. I got everything booked. Just got off the phone with Big Blue and Big Vic. Them and they security dudes, going to be waiting on you in 30 minutes at the airport. "Okay, Jacorius that's what's up! I got it." Said Dee-dee. Her and about 10 more girls was about to fly to Vegas. First class to attend an adult entertainment award show. Showing other exotic entertainers' support! After that, they were booked to hit a big strip club out there and then Saturday a bachelor party, for some folks in the porn industry! Sunday, another club in Cali. Jacorius didn't really have to travel with the girls anymore, unless he just chose to do so. He let Dee-Dee be the road manager for that. Besides, if he went, Dee-Dee would be all over him, trying to fuck his brains out! But blocking on sly slide at the same time! Jacorius had called back yesterday in exactly an hour like she wanted. She spoiled! They talked about all type of stuff. Family, kids, sex! Yea sex! It seems like Lashawn was ready, but hesitant. No pressure! She was his trophy! So, he was okay with the wait. She was on his mind, so he decided to call her.

They had gone through there morning ritual. He texts her faithfully every morning around 6:00. Or he would wake up, with a text on his phone from Lashawn. Where she had texted me at 1:30 a.m. or 3:00 a.m. Those times that she couldn't sleep, with a lot on her mind. Out of concern for her, Jacorius would make sure he sees about her as soon as he can! Either when he gets up in the morning or if he is up out and about. He gets back at her ASAP. Lashawn phone rings about five times. No answer. Now he's getting worried! For what? Jacorius actually felt for Lashawn and cared about her. He left her a voice message. "Lashawn... I don't know what's up, I hope everything is all right! But you got me worried about you! If everything is all right, you need to get at me ASAP! After Jacorius left the message, he got up and lit his cigarette and started pacing aimlessly through the house. After a couple of minutes, he thought about it... "She could be busy man, you are tripping!" Nevertheless, he still texts her a "What's up?" No response. What actually got him worried is Lashawn had a headache, early this morning and he got her to check her blood pressure, and it was a little above normal. He knew she had left work early and went home to relax. So, he was getting spooked! Thinking, what if she had fell out or something? There's nobody there to check on her. Maybe that nigga, done came home and tripping! "Let me calm down! My mind running wild!" Just as the thought hit him, his phone rung! It was Lashawn!

"Hello!" "Hey, how you doing?" Asked Lashawn. "I'm doing okay. Woman..." said Jacorius in a calm scolding way. You had me worried! You, okay?" "Yeah!" Laughs Lashawn. "I'm at the bank with my mother. I couldn't answer right then when you called, because I was talking to one of the bank personnel, trying to straighten some business up, with the bank and my mother. But... I listened to your voicemail, and I said Aww! He worried about me! You do care about me then!" Said Lashawn. "Yeah, I was worried about you! I care! You didn't answer the phone and that wasn't normal, especially when you were telling me earlier, that you weren't feeling good. "What you thought, I had fell out or something?" Laughs Lashawn. "Exactly!" "I'm doing okay." Said Lashawn. "My sister, I believe I did something slick, with my mama's money! They already trying to put in her head, that I'm doing something crooked against her, so we down here getting it straight!" Lashawn proceeded to fill Jacorius in on what was going on with the situation. About her sister using credit cards in which the money is being deducted, from their mama's bank account and so on. Lashawn had let Jacorius into her inner circle, so telling him things what was going on with her didn't bother her. She knew that he truly had her back, and she had his. They shared majority of all their problems.

A couple of weeks prior, Lashawn's mother has been in the hospital back-to-back! On two separate occasions, Jacorius showed support by calling her and staying on the phone with Lashawn, as long as she needed him. He talked to her and listened to her and tried to be as soothing as possible. Hours at a time! Never too busy for her, showing the quality attention and time, she needed. Something Robert wasn't doing. "I'm glad everything is okay!" said Jacorius. "Thanks! We're about to handle everything and get to the bottom of this! "I know that's right! How is Mama doing?" "She is doing okay." "That's good." "Look... Let me get back at you later, here comes the woman at this bank, I need to talk to." "Okay Lashawn, get back at me." They exchanged their goodbyes and Jacorius was sitting back, thinking how much he really cared about Lashawn... So fast! Actually, they've been knowing each other over a year, and a half.

They've been acquainted enough, to have dialogue on the regular basis. It's just the fact; he was feeling her on another level. Now that Jacorius had squared some legal business up, now it's time to square up some illegal business! His other phone has been jumping like a chat line. So, he got back at those people, now It was time to make a couple of plays. Drug deals, for those who don't know. Jacorius still sold X pills by the big sacks, all kinds of Kush weed by the pounds! and now big sacks of Oxycodone, and K4 Dillatas! White folk drugs! After going and making the plays he had lined up he put that money up at his stash house he had, he went and changed cars. He was about to take it and get it washed for his date tonight! On his way to the car wash, he called up this woman he knew named Renee to meet him at the car wash. Renee was a chick he met a while back when he was working at the college. He fucked her a couple of times, but it was nothing to them but friends. He was going to get her to come pick him up and ride him around and make a few more plays and probably smoke a little Purp with her. Until they got through with his car. And after that, to the crib take a bath and get ready for tonight!

Lashawn and her mother had left the bank about 30 minutes after talking to Jacorius. Lashawn was almost pissed, after finding out what had been going on with her mother's money. "Mama, you done worked all your life, and you got Daddy's pension coming to your account also. Now... How is it that after getting all that money a month, you don't have nothing in that account?!" "Lashawn, I don't even know!" Said Lashawns mother. "I just want you to make it, to where I have some money in my pockets." "Mama all your bills get paid, and we take you grocery shopping and whatever else you need. So, why would you want to be just sitting on money over there like that?" Lashawn already knew that her siblings were behind a lot of this drama, so she just kind of nipped the conversation in the bud, by grabbing her phone and calling Jacorius, to let him know that she has left the bank now. Besides, she needed to talk to him, to calm down. Her therapy.

Jacorius had just made three big plays and now was riding with Renae, smoking when his phone rung. It was Lashawn! "Damn! Should I answer this?" "Who is that your girlfriend?" Asked Renae smiling. "Well... Kind of sort of. Not yet." said Jacorius. "Damn! What kind of answer was that?!" Jacorius ignored Renae and was looking at his phone. What had Jacorius hesitant, was the fact that Lashawn didn't like for him to smoke! Cigarettes or weed. Then he didn't want her to get the wrong idea, when she heard Renae's voice, because he was feeling Lashawn for real, and was trying to knock her off! That is, make her his own! Then too, another thought kicked in... "I'm grown!" Said Jacorius. He respected Lashawn, but they weren't official...Yet. Jacorius answered the phone. "Hello?" "Hey!" Said Lashawn. "What's up? Everything all right? Turn that down" said Jacorius, referring to the radio. "Yeah, everything is all right." Said Lashawn in a skeptical way.

"Who are you talking to? Telling to turn the radio down?" "Oh, that's a friend. Just riding with her till they get through washing my car." "A friend? OH!" said Lashawn. "What?" Laughed Jacorius. "It's nothing. Straight up!" "Okay. Anyway." Lashawn proceeded to tell Jacorius what was going on, as him and Renae Rode and smoked until she heard him coughing. "Now wait a minute.. What you got a cold or something?" Asked Lashawn. Jacorius laughed it off. "No... I'm all right." "Okay. How many today?" Asks Lashawn. "I mean both!" "Well... A couple of blunts and about six or seven cigarettes!" "What! I bet your lungs just screaming!" Lashawn always kept up with how many cigarettes Jacorius smoke. "I'll slow down." "Anyway..." Lashawn started back telling Jacorius what was going on.

Chapter 14 (SPLIT)

She had dropped her mother off and Renae had dropped Jacorius off to get his car. They talked all the way up to both of them had them made it home. "What you fixing to do?" "About to take a bath What's up?" "Oh, nothing, probably gets some much-needed rest... What's up?" "Damn!" "What?" Asks Lashawn. "I thought you was going to say, pick me up Jacorius!" "Not yet... Sorry." Said Lashawn. "Yeah." said Jacorius in a sad way. "Don't say it like that!" "No, I'm cool." laughed Jacorius. "Well look, let me go ahead and get this bath." "Okay, call me later. I'll probably be up later on tonight." said Lashawn. "That's what's up!' As they hung up, Jacorius was putting money up and getting clothes out to wear for his date with Latonya. Knowing he wasn't going to call Lashawn back, but she still was on his mind. He'll make it up to her!

After Jacorius took a long bath and smoked a mini cigarillo, got dressed in some white linen, by Versace and some Gators by Mauri. Not to mention his favorite gold Rolex and diamond pinky ring! And Versace frames! Not the old kind, the new ones. Trying not to overdo it, but the kind of dude Jacorius is he likes to jump sharp and rep! Jacorius called Latonya to see was she ready and she was! "Okay, I'm on my way!" "Okay Jacorius," said Latonya. Jacorius grabs his keys and phone and was out the door, headed to the Jag. When Jacorius pulled up to Latonya's apartment at 7:00 p.m. on the dot, it's like she was already coming out the door! He didn't have to blow or nothing. She had to be looking out the window! And when Jacorius seen her, the first thing hit his mind was Trey Songz hit song "Making Love Faces!" It's like he was looking at Latonya in slow motion, as she came down the stairs and was headed to his car. The first part of love faces, when Trey Songz be talking about, imagining all the love faces the woman he is talking to could be making and when the beat drops and Trey goes to singing! "Love, love, love, love!" Is what's playing in Jacorius mind! Latonya has on all black, tight fitting strapless body dress, which is complimenting her every curve! It's made out of that shiny black material, as if they're going to a ball or something! Jacorius snaps out of his trans and gets out the car to greet her.

"Wow!" Said Jacorius as he approaches Latonya and hugs her. "Hey Jacorius!" Said Latonya as she blushes. "Damn you look great!" Said Jacorius as he spins Latonya around, by her hands to admire her. "Thank you! You don't look too bad yourself!" "I try!" said Jacorius. Then both of them laughs, because they both know that Jacorius is mocking Latonya! "Shall we?" Asks Jacorius as he opens the passenger door for Latonya. "Oh! A gentleman!" Said Latonya. "All the time Latonya, all the time!" said Jacorius as he closed the door and looks deeply into Latonya eyes, staring. "What?" Asks Latonya. "Damn what color are they now?" Referring to her eyes. "Oh, they're the same. Light brown! I don't have any contacts in." "Okay! You know it's hard to tell at times." said Jacorius. "Yeah, right! Come on Jacorius, Let's go!" smiles Latonya. When Jacorius and Latonya first started to get acquainted, off and on he used to talk about her eyes, knowing the outcome when you compliment a woman on something about her, besides the obvious. "Okay top down or up?" Asks Jacorius. "Oh, this is a convertible!" Said Latonya. "Yes, it is!" "You can leave it up." "Okay." said Jacorius as he crunk the Jag up and crunk the system up. Not loud. Just enough to hear the music and talk.

He had no other choice but to put on Trey songs, "Love Faces" and pulled off! At the same time as Jacorius was pulling off with Latonya, Lashawn was just waking up from her nap and instantly went for her phone, checking messages and so forth. Most of them she deleted them. Text and voice mails except the voice message Jacorius had left her earlier. She replayed it and listened to it about three times and then she sent him a text message. [Hey you! What's up?] Jacorius was in a small conversation with Latonya when Lashawn's text came through. He had his phone on him, he didn't want to seem disrespectful, but he still eases his phone out as Latonya was talking and checked it. "Go ahead and check that text or call! I ain't tripping!" said Latonya, with a smirk on her face. "No... It isn't like that Latonya. Just didn't want to seem disrespectful." "Yeah. Right!" Said Latonya. "I don't think you're being disrespectful, because I checked mine!" Raising her phone. He smiled and opened his text. It was a text from Lashawn. He read the text and decided to hit her back later on. "Everything cool?" Asked Latonya.

"Yeah, I'm Gucci!" Said Jacorius. "Why I be hearing folks say that?" "Say what?" asked Jacorius. "I'm Gucci!" Mocked Latonya. "Come on now, you know what that means!" Said Jacorius laughing. "What? Like you straight or something?" "Exactly!" Answered Jacorius. "Okay! I just don't want you to get in no trouble." Latonya said, with a sexy/ seductive smile on her face. Returning Latonya, a small sexy smile, laced with seduction! Jacorius was looking Latonya deep in her soul, dick getting hard! He wants to pull right over, off 95, and fuck her like they're on a porno flick! "That's my middle name. Trouble! You ain't no?" Latonya busted out laughing, playfully pushing his shoulder. "I hear you!" said Latonya. They continued talking and flirting, as they pass through Mims, headed to Palm Bay, to a little fly restaurant down there. Then after that, he was going to take her to this club in Melbourne Beach. A grown and sexy type of club. He figured 100 miles south of Daytona, Beach, would be nice and ducked off enough for her. He already had reservations at the restaurant and a hotel on the beach. Oh, it was going down!

Chapter 14 (SPLIT) (SPLIT)

It had been 30 or 40 minutes since Lashawn texted Jacorius. She was getting antsy now! "I ought to just call him!" said Lashawn. As soon as she said it, her phone rung, it was Robert! Rolling her eyes as she answers the phone. "Hello?" "What up?" Asks Robert. "Nothing." "Are you dressed?" "Dressed for what?" 'Come on now Lashawn! I told you yesterday, that I was going to take you out to eat tonight after I get off work." Sucking her teeth. "How many times, have I heard you say that, and you have to work later something?" Asks Lashawn. 'So... You're not dressed?" Asked Robert. "No." "Well. If you don't mind, could you put on something? Because we do, need to go out like we used to." Lashawn sat there thinking for a couple of seconds before she answered. "Okay Robert. I'm getting ready." "Good! It ain't got to be nothing fancy LaShawn". "Okay Robert, I'm getting up now." Said Lashawn. "Okay baby, bye." As Lashawn got up from her couch, she called Jacorius. After about five rings, his voicemail came on and she left him a message. {Hey Jacorius! I just woke up about 30 to 40 minutes ago, I text you... Oh well, just leaving you a message, about to go out to eat, I guess we'll talk tomorrow... Bye.} Lashawn hung up the phone and stood there a minute, wondering where Jacorius was! And what he was up to. "Oh, I got to get to moving!" She went and got a pair of jeans and a nice buttoned-down shirt, got dressed. She had already bathed before she took her nap. As she was getting herself together, she was catching all type of vibes from Jacorius! "Man, I wonder where you're at and what are you doing!"

Chapter 14 (SPLIT) (SPLIT) (SPLIT)

Jacorius and Latonya were in Palm Bay, at a restaurant, when his phone was ringing. He had put it on vibrate so it wouldn't be much of a disruption. Latonya had excused herself to the Ladies room. Probably checking her phone too! Jacorius pulled his phone out and seen the missed call from Lashawn. "Damn! I missed my baby!" Jacorius said to himself. He looks towards the lady's room, to see was Latonya coming back, so he could listen to the voicemail and sneak a quick text in. {Hey Lashawn! Sorry I missed your call, kind of tied up right now, and catch you tomorrow!} Just as he texted Lashawn, Latonya was coming out of the lady's room. As soon as she sat down, the food they had ordered arrived and they commenced to eating, talking, and laughing.

Just as Lashawn was reading your Jacorius's text, Robert came in the house. "You ready?" "Yes, I'm almost there!" said Lashawn as she was closing her text and putting the phone in her purse. "Who was that?" asked Robert. "A friend." said Lashawn with attitude. "I don't ask you, who you be talking to when you leave the room to talk on the phone." "Okay Lashawn whatever! Look we're going to have a nice time tonight without the arguing, Okay?" "Yeah, I hear you!" said Lashawn. Robert stood there, laying against the door frame, watching Lashawn and rubbing his head, like he's trying to figure something out. "What's wrong?" asked Robert. Lashawn stopped in mid-step. "Nothing! What's supposed to be wrong? "I mean... You been acting so funny and distant." Said Robert. She gave him a look like: "You don't know!" look and walks past him, turning off the light to the bedroom. "Hormones Robert! Let's go." Robert shook his head and followed Lashawn out the door.

By now, Latonya and Jacorius were through eating and was headed over to Melbourne Beach, to the club having a little small talk. Latonya checked her phone, as though it had just vibrated. "Everything cool?" Asks Jacorius. "Yeah. I'm good. I'm Gucci!" They both started laughing. "Just want to make sure you aint in no trouble!" said Jacorius. Latonya looked at Jacorius, smiling, "No... But my middle name isn't trouble!" Said Latonya. "I know! You are a good girl!" "That's right!" Laughs Latonya. They talked for the next 10- 15 minutes, until they pulled up at the club. They got in the club with ease, sat down and ordered their drinks. "What you're drinking?" Asks Jacorius. "Do they got Patron Silver?" "I'm sure they do! Let me ask the waitress. Excuse me, do y'all sell Patron Silver?" "We sure do sir!" Said the waitress. "Bring me the whole bottle and some cranberry juice!" Oh, bring two glasses of crushed ice." Latonya had an astonished look on her face.

"Now who going to drink all of that? You know that stuff strong! Oh, I get it. You trying to get me drunk!" "No!" laughed Jacorious. "I wouldn't do you like that! I'm drinking too!" "I know! I hope you going to be able to drive!" Said Latonya. "I got it. Don't worry." By that time, the waitress came back with the Patron and Cranberry juice. Jacorius gave her the money, paying for their drinks. Grabbing the liquor, the glasses, and the juice commenced the pouring up! "Hold up!" Said Latonya. "What's up?" Asks Jacorius, Frozen in mid-air, about to pour Latonya's drink. "Put about... That much liquor, and this much juice." Said Latonya imitating with her fingers. "Gotcha!" said Jacorius, obliges to Latonya's request. "Okay... That's straight." said Latonya. Then Jacorius poured his. "Okay let's make a toast!" Said Jacorius. "A toast to what?" said Latonya. "A toast to me, trying to get you drunk!" Latonya started laughing. "I'm not going to toast that! Let's toast to progression, in our friendship." said Latonya. Jacorius was smiling and looking deep in Latonya's eyes. "I'll go for that!' And they bumped glasses and sipped. Jacorius was a great actor. When he wants to be. True, he was into Latonya at the moment, but his mind was on Lashawn!

Lashawn and Robert ordered the two for $20 at Applebee's. While they sat there and ate, Robert was doing most of the talking. Filling Lashawn in on what's been going on with him and his colleagues at work and so forth. Lashawn was a great actress, when she wanted to be. Because she was eating and showing signs of attentiveness, but her mind was everywhere! Like: "I wonder where and what is Jacorius doing? And I don't really want to be here." One of their friends was a marriage counselor had told her to give it a chance with Robert and she had called Robert and told her to be nice to Lashawn and take her out to dinner and talk. So, she was going to go along with the program, charade, etc. But really, her heart wasn't 100% in it! Robert was regular talking and all of a sudden, he just flipped in mid-air! "Lashawn, what the hell is wrong with you?!" "What? I know you didn't just cuss me!?" "Well, I'm sorry I didn't mean it like that, but damn baby! Here I am trying to have a nice dinner with my soon-to-be wife, and it seems like your mind is in space somewhere!" Robert had been living with her long enough, to know when she's not there. But she wasn't having it, especially somebody cussing at her!

She was trying to quit cursing herself. "Look... I tell you what. I'll just... I don't know." Reaching for her phone. "I'll just call my sister or somebody to come get me, because this isn't going to work!" said Lashawn. "Hold up baby! You don't have to do all of that! Can't we just talk about it? I mean. What is wrong?" "Look... Excuse me, I got to go to the ladies room." Said Lashawn as she smoothly walked off. "Lashawn! Wait!" Said Robert, but Lashawn just kept on walking. She went in the bathroom and posted up at the mirrors and looked at herself. With tears forming in her eyes. "Stop it!" She told herself. "I'm not going to cry!" Wiping the tears before they could fall. She called her God- Brother, after five or six rings the voicemail came on. Next, she called Jacorius. Same thing! No answer, voicemail. "I knew I shouldn't have called him! He said he was tied up at the moment, anyway." Lashawn stood there for a minute, and got herself together and walked out of the bathroom and went back to the table with Robert and he was on the phone! "I'm sorry...Could you take me home? Robert looked up as he hung up the phone. "Okay, if that's what you want." "Yes, I do!" Robert got up from his seat and they left.

By now Jacorius and Latonya was on the dance floor, into each other, tipsy and slow dancing, to an old school "R Kelly" song, "It Seems Like you ready." He felt his phone go off, but he couldn't answer. He was too busy kissing on Latonya's neck, ears, and shoulders, and softly spitting game to her. He got her going! "Damn! You are softer than Dr's cotton!" Said Jacorius, as he slowly rubs and softly squeezes Latonya's round, bow hips and ass. "Oh yeah?" "Yeah!" Answers Jacorius as he looks Latonya in the eyes and kisses her lips. That kiss turned into another. Then into a tongue kiss! "Umm!" moans Latonya, as she smiles. "So you're a kisser." Jacorius kissed her again. "Let's go! So, I can really show you how I play the kissing game!" "Where are we going?"

"To that resort, right down the beach!" "Oh yeah?" "Yeah! I already got a suite reserved." Said Jacorius. Latonya laughed. "So you were that sure? How you know I wouldn't have declined?" "I don't know! But one thing I do know. We grown!" Next thing you know, in the next five minutes, Jacorius and Latonya was busting up in the suite, at the resort, kissing, about to tear each other clothes off at the door!

On the ride home from Applebee's, Lashawn gave Robert the cold shoulder, the whole ride home! He was trying his best to get through to her, but she wasn't having it. She was fed up! At least almost. While Robert was talking, Lashawn's phone rung. Checking the caller ID, it was her oldest daughter, Lashundria. "Hey girl! What are you doing?" Asked Lashawn. As she answered the phone. "Hey Mama! I ain't doing nothing, just calling to let you know we are almost home!" "Oh yeah? I thought you was going to wait till next weekend and come home? I thought y'all had forgot how to get to Daytona, Beach Florida." Said Lashawn. "Nawl mama, come on! It ain't like that!" Laughs Lashundria. "Oh yes, it is like that! Yall don't never come home! Let me speak to your sister." Said Lashawn. She was so glad, that her daughters were coming home for the weekend! When they first left for college, Lashawn didn't know what she would do. Also, she was glad that they called at this moment, because she would hold them on the phone, until she got home, and she wouldn't have to talk to Robert!

Meanwhile, Jacorius was hitting Latonya from the back! Face down ass up! He already had come one time and now Latonya was about to bring the other nut up out of him! The way she was looking back at him, with her finger in a mouth, was about to drive him crazy! At this point, it seems as if her eyes were glowing in the dark! They are already golden light brown! Up on his tip toes, on the bed, Jacorius was in dog mode! Jooking up in Latonya like it was his last piece of pussy, he would ever get! Softly pulling Latonya's hair, then all of a sudden: "Arrgg!" Jacorius let out a Neanderthal grunt. At the same time, Latonya moans, "oh yes, shit!" They both had reached their climax and collapsed! There night was over.

When Lashawn got home, she still was on the phone with her daughters. A perfect way to deflect Robert's conversations. A perfect way to deflect him period! "Lashawn. Are we going to finish our conversation?" "Hold on girl." she was walking in the house. "What conversation?" "Come on Lashawn, Don't play crazy. You know what I'm talking... "That conversation is over with, as far as I'm concerned!" Interrupts Lashawn. Robert stood there for a second or two, looking at Lashawn and turned around and walked back out the door! She wanted to throw her phone at him! "Momma! Are you okay?" Asks her daughter. "Yeah! I'm okay." Said Lashawn. "Well, I'll be up waiting on y'all! You know we got to have some girls talk!" "Okay Mama! We're almost there." "Okay." said Lashawn and hung up the phone and went in poured her a glass of wine and turned the TV on. Her mind was in overdrive! This relationship with Robert, it wasn't working! Point blank. She thought about Jacorius and what was he doing! She almost text him, but she said she would wait till tomorrow.

Chapter 15

JACORIUS AND LASHAWN

A couple of months had done passed, Lashawn and Jacorius relationship, well romantic friendship was getting deeper. Her relationship with Robert was definitely on the rocks! She knew that he was cheating but giving him the benefit of the doubt of not actually catching him, she was kind of holding on! Lashawn was not a temporary girl, so when she was in a relationship, she kind of latches on, and hopes that it would last a lifetime! Jacorius, on the other hand, had been used to running through women! But he did like the idea, of a lasting relationship... Probably marriage! Going steady, main girl, wifey, bottom broad thing, was a line he was kind of scared of crossing and was confused about! Yet, he wasn't getting any younger and when he was in prison, his mother preached the point of companionship. His relationship with Latonya was kind of on the rocks because, like Neecy, she still was kind of playing them X Games. Ex-boyfriend that is! Actually, she was having problems with him and Jacorius didn't want them problems! And she was kind of demanding! Besides, Jaco-rius came to his senses and find out that he really was just infatuated with Latonya, and wanted to see, how it was to sex her! Now that he had experienced sex with her, he realized he didn't have any deep feelings for her. True, he liked her, but his innermost feelings were aimed in a different direction... Lashawn!

He had to admit, he was really feeling her! The telephone conversation had gotten deeper. There meetings at Henrietta's, had become more frequent. He knew what he felt for Lashawn was real, when one day he was coming out of the bathroom, at Henrietta's, he saw her hug one of the cooks there, by the name of Rico and something ran through him like lightning! He had to turn around and go and sit down and get himself together! "Damn!" said Jacorius to his self, as he got it together. "What am I doing? She ain't my woman... I'm sitting here jealous." Knowing that she's friendly like that! All touchy, feely and that it might not mean nothing. But nevertheless, he was jealous of her! "I'm tripping!" Said Jacorius, as he got up and returned to his seat with Lashawn. Lashawn immediately picked up the vibe that Jacorius was giving off. "What's wrong with you?" Asked Lashawn. They were so connected, that either one of them knew when something was up with the other! "Nothing." Said Jacorius, putting a fake smile on his face. "Are you sure?" Jacorius pauses for a couple of seconds before answering and grabbing his phone at the same time. He decided to go ahead and address it and tell her what was on his mind! "I'm okay. But check this out... Something ran through me, when I saw you hug that nigga, Rico! I mean... I have seen you hug him before! In fact, I done seen you hug a couple of these cats! I know that's you and I can't be tripping, but... No lie, that got to me then! I don't know... I am not, no jealous dude. Well, I am a little... But not to the point of being crazy and shit... But... I don't know!" The whole time Lashawn was calm, but kind of surprised! She leaned back in her chair with a sly smile on her face, lowering her eyes. "Do you actually think that I would do something with Rico?! Matter of fact, do you think I would do something with any of these guys, you see me hug around here?" asked Lashawn, motioning with her hand towards empty chairs for effect. Jacorius shrugging his shoulders, with a lazy smile on his face, and said, "I don't know!" With that being said, Lashawn frowned at Jacorius and Smiled.

"I can't believe you said that!" In a calm, but rebuking kind of way. "I mean, Rico, Bobby, Marvin and whoever else you see me hug around here, I look at them as scrubs! I look at you to be more than them!" "Oh yeah?" said Jacorius. "Yeah!" said Lashawn. "I mean. Who I don't hug, is more of a threat to me, than them!" Now, with Lashawn saying that, Jacorius felt a little better, but he still had to edge it on a little bit. "So... You saying that's why you never hug me? That's why I can't never take you out?" "Yeah!" Answered Lashawn. "I'm trying to be good in my situation." "Lashawn, I can only go as far as you let me."said Jacorius. "And that's the thing... How you know, I won't let you go, as far as it can go? I thought I told you one time, that you like my kryptonite!" said Lashawn. "Hold up! You need to turn it down a little bit!" Laughs Jacorius. "What? I'm serious!" said Lashawn. Jacorius kind of felt, where she was coming from. Truth be told, Jacorius was wondering why he was still playing along with this charade, but he knew in his heart, why he was... He wanted Lashawn badly! They truly had each other's back! And that made him feel good. To know that a woman, really had his back and that he truly had a woman's back! Other than for getting paid or sex. They had a real connection! The only thing Lashawn wanted Jacorius to do besides, quitting smoking, was to stop hustling! He didn't know, how she knew, but she had brought it up a couple of times. She knew he had his own business going, with the strippers and was somewhat involved in day trading stocks and mutual funds, but her instincts told her more! Jacorius was sitting around the crib, thinking about all of this, when his phone rung. It was Lashawn! He knew she wasn't on her break, because it was only 11:00 a.m. "What's up?" said Jacorius answering the phone. "Hey, how you doing?" said Lashawn in a rushed tone. "I'm cooling, what's up? You all right?" asked Jacorius.

He could tell something was wrong. "It's my mama... Again!" "Is she okay? asks Jacorius as he jumped up and put his tennis shoes on. About a week prior, Lashawn's mother was admitted to the hospital and Jacorius had put everything to the side and talked to Lashawn all day, and through the night off and on showing her support. "I don't know Jacorius is she okay or not. She called Robert first and he called me. Then just as I was about to call her she called me saying: "I'm dying Lashawn, I'm dying!" So, my brother called the ambulance, and now I'm leaving work headed to the hospital!" "Okay, Lashawn, I'm on my way." said Jacorius. "No... you don't have to come. Just stay on the phone with me, Okay?" "Lashawn, you sure? You know I got you." "Yea, Yea I'm okay, just talk to me." So, Jacorius did just that, as Lashawn entered the emergency room and talked to the doctor and nurses in charge. "Jacorius you still there?" "Yea baby, I'm still here, I am not going nowhere."

"Good!" said Lashawn. "Hold on." Listening to Lashaun background, Jacorius could tell that she was talking to her brother... "I'm back," said Lashawn. "OOO! I can't stand Ced!" "Where is he?" asked Jacorius "Out here in the parking lot, begging folks for cigarettes! I'm back in my car now." "Okay Lashawn, be easy on your brother. He might be nervous." said Jacorius. "Yeah right!". Jacorius talked to Lashawn, all day while she was at the hospital. When they brought her mother to her room, after running some tests on her, she was all right, thank God! He was on the phone, as she was talking to the doctor and her mother. She might have told him to call her back once or twice or she would call him back, but he kicked it with her all day and that night. Even as he went and handled business in the streets, he still held her down. "You hungry?" Jacorius asked Lashawn, after he had just gone and made a play. "Yeah." "What you want?" "Something from Zaxby's will do." "Bet!" He went to Zaxby's and got her Chicken tenders, fries, salad and a large, sweet tea. "I know you probably don't want me to come in the hospital, where are you parked at?" asked Lashawn. She told him where she was parked. Lashawn made her way out the hospital and headed to her car. "Where you at?" asks Jacorius. "I'm at my car?" answered Lashawn.

"Ok. I see you. Is it cool to pull on up? I mean, your situation isn't here is he?" Asks Jacorius. "No." said Lashawn. "He said he had to work over. I don't know... I don't care! Wait a minute... How you see me? Where you at?" asks Lashawn. Proving her suspicious right, Jacorius pulled right up on her! In his new infinity truck, Q56 2025 model. It was a shiny platinum color, with some big rims on it. "Right up on ya!" said Jacorius, smiling, as he pulled up and jumped out, with Lashawn's food in his hand. "How are you feeling?" asks Jacorius as he hands Lashawn her food. "I'm good!" said Lashawn smiling. "You are so sweet! Oh... And who truck is this?" "Oh, this me! Just got it yesterday. You like it?" "Yeah! It's pretty." Said Lashawn. "But... I ain't in your business. But whatever you are doing. If it ain't right, you need to slow down." Jacorius knew Lashawn cared about him, just as much as he cared for her. So, he wasn't going to come off all sideways on her. Then he had much respect for her, so he just took what she said in stride. "Okay... I hear you!" said Jacorius, smirking. "You are smiling, but I'm for real!" said Lashawn.

"Okay... Consideration taken. But you are looking good as always!" said Jacorius. Swiftly changing the conversation. "Thank you! But you think you're smart!" said Lashawn. They both laughed. They talked for about 5 minutes, and Jacorius left. The conversated over the phone, about 3 hours later, when Jacorius got home. They both went back to their high school days. Going to sleep on the phone on each other, talking to the next morning almost! Lashawn had stayed all night, with her mother at the hospital. Sleeping on a foldaway bed. Lashawn's mother was in the hospital for three more days and it was the same routine they already had and more. Jacorius made sure he checked on her, in person at least twice a day, and they talked and text all day! Jacorius was meeting the basic needs, a married, or almost married woman, is lacking from their current spouse. He showed Lashawn genuine affection. He was so caring that she yearns and aches for Jacorius!

To the point, to where she even told him that. That was another need he fulfilled, honesty and openness, and she enjoyed his conversation. Those are the top three basic needs a man would need to know, to keep their marriage or relationship, affair free. That's if he has a good woman and she's not a straight up slut bucket or whore, or freak! Jacorius relationship with his other women, was basically on the rocks. A fuck here and there, but that was basically it. Is Cocoa look alike, Jan, the rich white woman, he still fucked her heavily, because she contributed to his hustle and his lifestyle. But he didn't have any feelings involved, plus she had a life with her husband. He was so involved with Lashawn, that when she wanted to know who her competition was, he told her about Jan! "A white woman!?"

Lashawn almost screamed! Jacorius told her how that came about, and a little about the others, but assured her that she had his feelings. "What other dude do you talk to like you talk to me?" Jacorius asked once, to settle his suspicions and to make sure that she was meeting him on the 50! Halfway. "Nobody!" Lashawn answered. And Jacorius believed her, for some reason. He cared for her. So, whatever. "Look." said Lashawn, "I done told you that you're in my spirit now, and you have gotten close to me, very close to me! Which I don't really let happen, and how it happened I don't know!" "Oh yeah?" Jacorius interrupted. "Yeah!" said Lashawn. "Let me finish. Okay?" "Go ahead." said Jacorius. Smacking her lips, in a girly way, as she continued. "Anyway... I guess, you just had to be so caring, attentive, and not judgmental, to my rantings and raves." "And I told you, you got me in whatever capacity you need and want me in!" said Jacorius. "Yeah, yeah, I know!" Said Lashawn. But... Look. You going to have to leave that white woman alone!" Jacorius started laughing. "I'm serious!" said Lashawn. "A white woman?! I mean... Whatever you were using her for, it looks like you done accomplished your goal. So... For our sake. Please! Okay?" "Okay... I hear you." Laughed Jacorius.

"It's really not that serious. My relationship with her. But... What about your situation?" asked Jacorius. "What about my situation? You already know that it's not working out! Just hold on. Bear with me." "Bear with you?" Asks Jacorius. "I mean... How long I got to do that?" Lashawn had got quiet. She was thinking 100 mph. She hasn't told Jacorius that she was engaged to Robert! "You there?" asks Jacorius. "I'm here. Just thinking... Like I said, let things flow, if it's meant to be, it will be." Said Lashawn. "Okay. I hear you." said Jacorius. "You still got my back?" asks Lashawn. "Yeah. For Life!" said Jacorius. At that point they changed the subject. Jacorius knew that Lashawn wanted to leave Robert, but she wanted everything to be secure. He was security! But Jacorius could be security to her, but she knew the lifestyle he lived was dangerous! One day you're here and the next day you're gone! And she knew he had plenty of women! So, she had to work on Jacorius a little more. He was a street dude. A gangster! Even though he has gotten older, but she seen it in him, which is exciting, but she didn't want to wind up getting hurt. It was a challenge for the both of them. Her, trying to almost change him, and him trying to get her to cross in line in which he knows she wants to cross, but was very hesitant! A couple of weeks had done flew by. Jacorius had been out of town, tending to business.

The whole time, he's been communicating with Lashawn, sticking to their regular schedule. All day! Lashawn had been sharing with Jacorius what had been going on with her. She was going through some rough times, and she was sick of looking at her friends. They're always there when they need something, but she couldn't seem to find them when she needed something! She assured him not to worry about it and that she's been in there before. Lashawn knew that she had to remove those seasonal people. Being the faithful person, she is, she believed God would send some more good friends. Lashawn knew, every once in a while, in life, a lifetime friend will pop up, like Jacorius! They both confessed to each other, to be lifetime friends and that they both had each other's back! Jacorius called Lashawn, just as soon as he came in from Atlanta. "Hello?" answered Lashawn. "Hey, how you doing?" said Jacorius. Lashawn letting out a sigh of relief. "Oh terrible!" "Terrible?" Asks Jacorius. "You sound stressed." "I am!" said Lashawn and went on to tell Jacorius what was going on with her. "Look... I'm not taking no for an answer! Let me take you out and away for a few days, you'll be straight!" Said Jacorius. Normally, Lashawn would have been worried about everybody else and work, but she was at the end of her rope. Pausing a couple of seconds before answering.

"Okay!" Said Lashawn. "Okay... Give me 20 minutes. That's cool?" said Jacorius. "Perfect!" said Lashawn. They exchanged their goodbyes, and Lashawn grabbed her carry-on bags and threw a few items in the bags and got ready to leave. in exactly 10 minutes, Jacorius was there! Lashawn was on the porch waiting. Jacorius got out of the car and the first thing he did was hugged Lashawn! Wrapped her up in those big strong arms and just let her lay her head on his shoulders. Lashawn felt so safe and secure. Felt like all was okay. Jacorius grabbed her bags and told her to get in the car and just relax. "Where are we going?" asked Lashawn. "It's a surprise. Be cool!" She leans back and they left. Jacorius was driving a metallic green Mustang... 5-speed! Lashawn, she just loved that sports car! If you don't ride her on his red motorcycle, a Hibachi. Jacorius and Lashawn were riding through the cities and headed out of it. Lashawn started to drift off to sleep, but not before they really hit the road. Jacorius places his hand on her thigh! Just that small gesture, brought so much comfort that Lashawn fell asleep. Just embracing her. The rhythm of his hand making circles. The music, "Johnny Gill" And just that he would take care of her, she finally fell asleep. Jacorius woke Lashawn up 2 hours later, to a beautiful park sitting in Pinella, outside of Tampa, where he had put everything together for a picnic.

Lashawn laid on the blanket and Jacorius lying beside her, feeding her fruit. But Lashawn needed more than fruits, and food. But Jacorius, took things at a comfortable pace. Lashawn ate and then snuggled closer in his arms. "You still haven't told me where we were going." Said Lashawn. "You'll see." said Jacorius. Lashawn felt her eyes getting heavy and Jacorious noticed. "Go ahead and rest Lashawn, I'm here and nothing or no one will bother you... I got you!" Lashawn fell asleep, with Jacorius kissing her eyes, to keep them closed. He let her sleep for about an hour, she was awakened to Jacorius, kissing her lips. Her whole body felt on fire! Jacorius could tell, that at that very moment, Lashawn was ready! But he still held back. Smiling, looking deep into Lashawn eyes, caressing her arms, and down to her hands, making small circles, in the palm of her hands. He raises her left hand and slowly raise the inside of her wrist, an inch below the bottom of her palm and gently kiss and nibble on it. Lashawn smiles and lets out a slow giggle. "What?" asks Jacorius, as he continues to slowly kiss, suck, and nibble on the inside of Lashawn's arm. She was so elated and surprised but yet turned on by Jacorius tenderness and affection. Her only answer to him was, "You are a mess!" "Oh yeah? Am I making a mess?" asks Jacorius as he run his fingers around Lashawn's ears. "What you think?" Said Lashawn. Jacorius laughs as he pulls Lashawn to her feet. He softly kisses her on the lips.

He starts getting all of their picnic stuff together and putting it in the trunk. "Now, I'm not taking no for an answer this time!" Laughed Lashawn. "Where are we going now?" "Just chill!" laughed Jacorius. They hopped in the car and pulled off. They talked for about 5 minutes as they rode south on 75. Jacorius hand was back on Lashawn's thigh, caressing it. She laid back and slept. In the next hour and a half, they were pulling up in Marcellus. They caught a boat out to Marco Island that evening and walked the beach, hand in hand. Lashawn's mind was reeling now! She hasn't received this type of affection in a long time! They walked, talked, and laughed. Jacorius got behind her and massaged Lashawn's neck and shoulders, as they watched the sunset. "You ever wonder about, the view behind the ocean?" Lashawn eyes had been closed, enjoying the massage. She opened them now and looked... "Yeah. I have. What's to wonder about that particular view Jacorius?" laughed Lashawn. "Everything!" said Jacorius. "The color, the way the sun looks like it just sitting on the ocean. If I told you, that I have the answer to space and the view behind the ocean, would you believe me?" Lashawn quickly looks back at Jacorius.

"You been smoking that stuff today too?" Laughs Lashawn. And where did you get that from? I mean, what you just said." "Scarface! The rapper. It was on a song, on the "Untouchable" CD." said Jacorius, as he still massages Lashawn. "Well... I don't listen to much rap." Spoke Lashawn. "It's something to think about though." Looking at the view behind the ocean, about an hour after dark, Lashawn and Jacorius went to the resort on the island and had a few drinks and talked. Jacorius went ahead and rented a suite. Truth be told, he was kind of tired and he knew Lashawn was winding down, so neither one of them would be fit to drive back. He knew that Lashawn probably had a little reservation about spending the night with him, but he surprised her. He let her sleep in the bed, and he slept on the lazy boy, next to the bed! Lashawn was confused! She knew that Jacorius wanted to have sex with her, and she knew that Jacorius knew that, right about now that she was ready! She almost got out of bed to go and see what was up with him! It's like he read her mind, because as soon as she lifted her head up, to see was he sleep, his eyes popped open looking dead at her! Making her jump! "Sleep Lashawn." said Jacorius.

"What?" said Lashawn. "Okay." She laid back down and took advantage of the moment and slept. Even though, it took her an hour to fight what she was feeling, away. Anticipation! She just knew Jacorius was going to get in the bed with her. But nevertheless, when she awoke the next morning, she wanted him more than ever now! Room service had brought them breakfast. They sat there and ate in silence... Well, their eyes were doing the talking for them, until Jacorius broke the silence. "What's up?" He asked. In a girly innocent tone, Lashawn answered: "I'm okay!" shrugging her shoulders at the same time. Jacorius actually wanted to dive over the table at her and just snatch her clothes off and make urgent, passionate love to her! But instead, he chills. "That's good." said Jacorius. Lashawn giggled, because she knows what was on Jacorius mind. A woman knows, when desire exists for her and when desire don't exist. She just wondered, why he was holding back! His patience and tenderness with her, earned him a lot of cool points and deposits in his account in her love bank! After they ate, Jacorius showered first and then Lashawn showered.

They got their stuff together and they rode out. Lashawn and Jacorius both had been ignoring their calls, all except the ones from family and friends in their inner circle. They both assured the ones who it matters to, that everything was okay, just a little getaway for some R&R. Gerald had called Lashawn that night and that morning, and she Let him know the same thing. He acted as if he couldn't understand, and wanted to know who she was with, but something was telling her that he was glad that she was away! So that he could play! "You alright?" asks Jacorius, as Lashawn hung the phone up from Gerald. "Yeah, I'm good." said Lashawn, with a frown on her face. "You sure?" "Yeah", laughed Lashawn. Putting on her happy mask. She didn't want Jacorius to worry, because she didn't want to ruin their fun. But they were united in spirit. Jacorius and Lashawn, so he felt it. Changing the atmosphere, Jacorious joked with Lashawn about her snoring. "I don't snore! That was you, I heard snoring. You know you been on the road, the last couple of days, you tired!" said Lashawn. They laughed and talked a couple of more hours, as they rode back up to Flagler Island. "Now... What you know about this place?" Lashawn skeptically asked Jacorius.

"What place? Flagler Beach / Island... The city of Flagler... What?" asks Jacorius. "Okay Mr. Smarty!" said Lashawn. As she playfully punches Jacorius in the shoulder. "I'm talking about Flagler period!" Jacorius didn't know that Lashawn owned a house on Flagler Island. "Well, I don't know much about it, I've been up here two or three times to the beach, that's about it! Why you ask me that? What you know about it?" said Jacorius. With a sly grin on her face, Lashawn said... "Maybe a little more than you... I take that back. More than you probably would think! Jacorius was looking at Lashawn, frowning with curiosity, written all over his face, as he drove to Flagler Beach. "Somebody done brought you up here before?" "No!" Laughs Lashawn. "Let's just say... When I want to get away... Especially when I go into my shell! I have a secret cave up here." Jacorius quickly looked at Lashawn, frowning and smiling. "A cave like you and I have talked and fantasized about?" Lashawn started laughing. "Maybe! We'll just have to see." "That's what's up!" said Jacorius

Chapter 16

LASHAWN'S CAVE

Jacorius and Lashawn had been on the beach, practically all day. It wasn't too hot and wasn't too cold. Typical Florida weather in November. They walked the beach and talked. Had a few moments where they wrestled and played like some kids. Even tried to build a sandcastle too! They went and had dinner, at a small restaurant on the beach, had a drink or two, and talked some more. "Want to go to my cave?" asked Lashawn, with a smirk on her face. "Why sure! I thought we were supposed to went there while we were walking the beach. You know. Like in our fantasy world when we go there, in conversation." said Jacorius. "Umm... Not exactly! Come on." said Lashawn, as she grabbed her purse and was rising out of her seat. Jacorius smiling, followed suit. Lashawn and Jacorius rode up the beach, about a mile and a half, passed some condos, which was mostly some time-shared properties, and slowed down. "What? You own one of these condos?" asks Jacorius. "No... You are almost there. Take the next left." said.

Lashawn. Jacorius took the left, driving slowly. Looking as if he was in awe, the scenery was intriguing him, to almost ask more questions, as they quietly rode passed brick walls, in which served as privacy fences, lined with palm trees and shrubs. After about a half a mile of riding, Lashawn spoke. "Take this right." Jacorius took the right and after passing about 10 houses, Lashawn spoke up. "Okay, take this left." Jacorius found himself turning into an iron gate. Lashawn rolled the window down and punched in the code and the gates swung open and closed behind them.

The driveway was about 50 yards long, was led to a nice one-story Bungalow home, surrounded by a brick privacy fence, which stood about 9 ft, with hedges every 3 ft within the walls. The walls stood taller than the fence. A few Palm trees, in the front and backyard, with a patio which allowed her to see the beach and ocean. "How do you like my cave?" asks Lashawn, as she giggles. "It's cool!" said Jacorius, as he got out of the car looking around. Jacorius grabbed their bags as Lashawn unlocked the door. Upon entering the house, Jacorius sat the overnight bags down, in the immaculate living room and started to looking around and admiring the whole downstairs layout. Jacorius was amazed! "Who did the interior design?" Lashawn stops what she was doing and placed her hand on her hips, acting as if she was offended. "Me!" said Lashawn, slowly pointing at herself for emphasis. Jacorius throwing his hands up in surrender, smiling. "My bad, my bad! I know you got that touch!" "Yeah, and you better not forget it!" Laughs Lashawn. "Oh, you want something to drink?" asks Lashawn, as she went to her small bar. "Yeah! Give me some Cîroc." said Jacorius, as he still was admiring Lashawn's interior design skills. The living room was laid!

She had a Lillian August furniture set, wrap around sofa and love seat, was Hickory White, with a thick black bear skin, spot rug covering a partial part of the off grayish, with an off-earth tone type of green. Hardwood floors, with the off gray painted walls, with a few random paintings and frame pictures of her! Lashawn brought Jacorius his drink. "You still admiring my work?" "Yeah!" "Don't you have some clothes that need washing in your bag?" asked Lashawn. "Matter of fact, I do." said Jacorius. "Well, I'm about to wash some stuff, you want me to add your stuff too?" "Yeah... That'll be cool!" Jacorius grabs one of his Louis, overnight bags and follows Lashawn to her laundry area. "Here..Dump them in there." said Lashawn, opening the washing machine. Jacorius dumped his clothes in the washing machine. Then Lashawn did the same, except she was putting clothes in from a dirty clothes hamper. "You must have been up here recently?" asked Jacorius. "Yeah! Me and my daughters came up here a couple of weeks ago. Then me and my girls, from the book club had a get together. Then, I've been up here a couple of times recently, by myself! Just to get away. Why you asked me that? You judging from these clothes I'm putting in here?" Smiled Lashawn. "Yeah!" "Go in the living room and relax. Turn on the TV." said Lashawn. "Will do!" said Jacorius, as he walked off, nursing his Cîroc. And went and did just what Lashawn told him to do! He grabbed the remote, turned on the TV and sat down and relaxed. Jacorius sat there sipping his drink and looking at ESPN, for about two or three minutes.

He pulled out his phone and went to the music app and turned on Johnny Gill and let it play. He decided he was going back in the washroom where Lashawn was. Thinking about a fantasy, she once told him about, that started when she was about 17. That thought, makes Jacorius get up and walk back to the washroom, after turning up his drink. Stepping back in the washroom, Jacorius stood there, admiring Lashawn's figure, no more than a couple of seconds, when Lashawn felt his presence. She looks back at him and smiles, and he approached. They were in the washroom, and she had so much to do but felt so much comfort, just being in his presence. She leaned back into his arms and laid her head on his chest. Their bodies molded together as one, they met in all the right places! She felt his warmth against her behind. It was full and caused her to think how it would feel, touching her core. She closed her eyes and relaxed in the warmth of his love, letting her desires be released. He ran his hands down to her arms, back up to her shoulders. Her breasts longed for the touch of his hands. He briefly ran his thumb across her nipples. She moans and lean more into his body. He became harder! But she knew he was holding back, trying to bring her some comfort, without putting pressure on her. He knew, how she had been used, by so many others and he did not want to be put into that category in her mind. So, he followed her lead, not knowing that she wanted him so badly, that she ached inside! She had to take things slow, because she wanted to savor every single moment that they were together! So, she moved away and went to pick up more clothes to place in the washing machine. He was watching her every move. And once she bent over, he could not help but touch her, caressingly on the behind. This touch caused her more moisture in the juncture of her thighs! She turned around, to look into his eyes and saw the darkness of lust in their depths.

She walked up to him, lacing her hands on his shoulders. The look she gave him, cause him to need more contact with her body, so he leaned in for a kiss. The moment their lips met; sparks begin to fly! At first, the kiss was soft, but as time passed, it became more deeper and more passionate. They finally had to release their hold and come up for air! "Umph!" moaned Lashawn, But the tension was there for them both and they knew that, if not today, then soon, they will have to do something, to put an end to the frustration, that was surrounding their bodies and the wanting they both felt. "What's up?" asked Jacorius. She knew they needed to talk, so she took his hand and led him through the kitchen, into the living room. She knows she needs to stop there, because down the hall, was the bedroom! And if she even started in that direction, she knew she would not be able to stop the desire from overtaking the last resolve, she had on her body. Because her body was telling her mind something different! She had to decide if she wanted to sit behind him on the sofa or across from him. In a chair. Sitting on the sofa will put her too close, and her emotion were so wired, that she just wanted him to take her and relieve her Tension!

She was starting to have aches in places she did not know could throb! She knew a fire was starting and only he could quench it! So, she sat across from him. She had to take a few breaths, just to get herself together. "You okay?" asks Jacorius, as he watches Lashawn as she tries to compose herself. "Yeah." said Lashawn. As she smiles and fans herself. Jacorius really wants her to move over to the sofa and sit next to him. He felt a loss without her closeness. She finally felt she could talk, without wanting to jump up and cross the room, straddle his body and just let him have his way! "Lashawn check this out." said Jacorius. "I'm letting you know now that I'll never ever take our friendship for granted. You feel me?" She watches him and believes that his words are true. "Yeah... Yeah, I feel you." They talked about their families and things that are happening in their lives. She was having problems with her family.

Concerning her mother and he thought his family was not there for him in his situation, backing him. She had recently talked to his mother and knew that his mother was trying to understand, but was having a hard time, so she told him. He was so happy that Lashawn was taking an interest in his personal life, and he loved her all the more! She saw the change in him and desire to be close, she crossed the room, to go into his arms! Jacorius held her close, and she feels so tired! "You know I haven't been sleeping well." said Lashawn. "And the fatigue is catching up with me!" "I know, but I'm here... I got you." said Jacorius. Lashawn felt herself nodding off as Jacorius caressed the small of her back. She succumbed to the feel of his hand and the love she felt radiating from his body. She finally had peaceful sleep, until her body took over! Because as she slept, she dreamed of him. And her dream had her really crossing over and getting fulfilled! As she slept, she moaned... The more Lashawn slept, the deeper she went into her dream! Not realizing that her dream, was about to be true life! Because Jacorius was watching her body and hearing her moans.

He touched her lips with his fingers and her moans were louder. He touched her breasts, as they rose with her breathing. She felt the touch and her body responded. His hands traveled lower and as he touched her abdomen, her eyes opened! Lashawn looked at Jacorius and the tenderness she saw in his eyes made her want him even more. He picked her up and laid her on the floor. The plushness of the carpet made her feel like she was laying on a bed of roses! He Lowered himself down beside her and pulled her into his arms. "Lashawn, I have waited patiently for this moment, but if you feel uncomfortable, I will gladly continue to wait. Because my love for you, is strong!" Lashawn smiles and lean in to kiss Jacorius. He placed his hands on her hips and pulled her in close, to feel the fullness of his body. She felt every inch and knew at that very moment, that she wanted him inside of her! He removed her top and slowly, undid her bra. She removed her hair clamp and let her hair cascade to her shoulders. She knew he loved the fullness of her hair. He removes his shirt, and she ran her hands over his chest, feeling the muscles ripple beneath her touch. As Lashawn is running her hands up and down his chest, feeling the ripples of his muscle, her desire is consuming her very soul, and her thoughts are only of him! As their lips meet, and the passion overtakes her and she deepens the kiss, to convey her feelings of want! He feels her and lowers his hands to her behind to bring her even closer. She feels as if, she has become a very part of him.

She feels his desire, as he rises, and she knows that at this very moment, she does not want to be anywhere else but in his arms. Jacorius caresses Lashawn in her most intimate parts and she feel the beginning of a release. A nut! Not sure if she wants it this way but she is powerless to stop the movement of his hands! She arches and as the movement continues the pressure builds within her more and more and more... And she explodes! As she lets off a deep Moan. Jacorious watches and realizes, this is what she needed more than anything. "You ready for more?" asks Jacorius. Lashawn just nods her head in the affirmative. She knows that he will bring her more pleasure in the forth coming hours. She has waited so long for this moment, and she wants to savor every second! By now, Jacorious reaches around and squeezes Lashawn's firm ass and slides Lashawn's panties and capris down. With her help, the panties and capris are off. And at this moment Jacorius is coming up out of his jeans and boxers. Kicking them off, along with his shoes.

All patience, between the both of them, quickly melts away, by the heat of their urgency and long withheld passion takes over! Jacorius quickly jumps between Leshawn's legs, with her grabbing his dick and placing it where it needs to be! Inside of her! Meeting each other's, immediate thrust, is the start of their mission to please. Lashawn wraps her strong legs around Jacorius waist, as if she never wants to let go. He puts both hands on the floor, gripping the thick carpet, looks Lashawn in the eyes as he grinds hard in circular motions and tongue kissing Lashawn as she wraps her arms around his neck. He stops tongue kissing her and starts sucking on her ears and neck, but not long enough to bruise her. He remembered that she said, she was a tender chick! LaShawn's coochie was so good to him, he almost came too fast! So, he slowed up and rolled her over, to where she was on top of him, to let her ride him. Lashawn was doing a great job at riding him! She started off just grinding on top of him with her hands in his chest, then she picked up the pace, as she was squeezing on the muscles in his chest, as he played with her breasts. Jacorius was caressing her side, her lower back, and her firm ass, squeezing it and pulling her by the shoulders, make her go into a frenzy as he pushed up into her harder!

Lashawn snatched his hand hands and pent them to the floor and grabbed the thick carpet at the same time and literally fucked Jacorius, to her eyes rolled like some slot machine numbers! She threw her head back and both of them reached their climax. Jacorius was still pumping, not wanting his erection to disappear, he quickly rolled Lashawn over and kept grinding and stroking in her. Lashawn assisting him by making the muscles in her pussy contract and grip his dick, as she was gripping his butt, pulling him up in her! He got all the way back hard... Quickly! That's when he pulled up out of her, snatched a seat off of the couch, put it up under her stomach, grabs her by her waist, as she arched her back and started hitting it from behind! "We Went to dinner and a movie and now we so ready!" Johnny Gill's old song Played softly in the background, as Jacorius and Lashawn experiments in sweaty sex! It's a trip, because it's a line that Lashawn said that she would never cross! That is, put herself in a compromising position, by being alone with Jacorius! In her own words: "Playing with fire!" "Oh, shit baby! Right there don't stop!" Moaned Lashawn. Jacorius obliges to Lashawn's request without a break in his stride, trying his best to break his dick off and lose it in Lashawn! At least that's what it seems like to Lashawn or if walls could see and talk, that's what they would say! But she's loving every minute of it! Because Jacorius is helping Lashawn relieve all pent-up tension and anxiety! And she is helping him alleviate pent up stress and tension. Even swap isn't a swindle! "Damn boo, you fucking me good!" said Jacorius be-tween gasps as he spontaneously spins her off of her stomach from the semi doggy style position to her back! Pushing her knees to her ears, invoking what he calls the love zone. Looking Lashawn deep in her eyes, he slows his pace yet lays the pound game on! Slow with a passion, then out of the blue, he deeply tongues Lashawn! Almost causing an eruption within seconds! Between the both of them! Moments get intense, Jacorius and Lashawn both speed up, meeting each other, halfway. Stroke for stroke pound for pound! Then, "Oh my God!" Screams Lashawn, as her and Jacorius reaches their climax at the same time!

Sparks fly! Lashawn shakes and makes the "Umph" sound, as Jacorius trembles and collapse on Lashawn, as he tries to catch his breath. "Told you to quit smoking!" said Lashawn, as she giggles at Jacorius, while he catches his breath. He lays between Lashawn beautiful brown thighs and slowly grinds in her. Caresses her, like her favorite song, Kelly Rowland's "Motivation!" Yeah, when she says, "hands all over me baby!" "Do you feel like you're being well kept?" asked Jacorius, as he run his fingers, both hands, through Lashawn's hair as he kisses her. A pregnant 5 second pause ensues between the two, as Jacorius and Lashawn exchange stares.

Jacorius smiles, breaking the silence. "Hello?" asks Jacorius. "I heard you." said Lashawn. "Let me ask you this: Do I come off as being temporary to you? Lashawn asks Jacorius. "No!" Laughs Jacorius. "We had this conversation not long ago, do you remember?" "Yeah! But do you remember what I told you?" asks Lashawn. Answering her own question, "And that is, I'm spoiled, I want what I want, when I want it! Now can you handle that?" "For sure!" smiles Jacorius. She knows Jacorius is a nice, caring man, who wants nothing from her, but to be there to hold and console her. He is so caring that he makes her body ache and yearn for him! But due to her situation, her career and engagement, and his position and lifestyle, is a line she didn't want to cross, unless she was sure and safe! But now she has crossed it!

CHAPTER TWENTY-ONE

Chapter 17

THE MORNING AFTER

Lashawn was sitting on the sofa, watching tv as Jacorius slept. She could not sleep! And she had a lot on her mind. How did she let him get in so fast? She usually had her guard up. What about Jacorius was so special? Why did she feel so comfortable around him? How did he get so far under her skin? She watched him more than the TV and she wanted to rejoin him! Awaken him and start all over again! But she had to contain herself, because she had some soul searching to do. She had never crossed this line, but things with Jacorius was different and she wanted it to be permanent! Because she was not a temporary girl. She needs to know if he was accessible to her needs. She was so tired of the runaround and shake down that she was currently getting, and her heart was hurting! She was in desperate need of tender loving care, that didn't just involve her doing everything and being sexed. She needed someone who understood her inner workings, without having to be told. She needed someone who gave just as much as she did and didn't always expect something from her in return.

She needed someone who just loved her, because no other reason! She wanted to be pampered. She had talked about this with Jacorius before, but she was unsure if he really understood how badly she needed these things. All her life she had been there for others and now she just wanted someone to be there for her. She knew it was time to discuss this again to the fullest. She crossed the room to turn on the radio and what would be playing, One of her favorite songs "Motivation!" by Kelly Rowland. She stopped and looked down at Jacorius and he was looking up at her. No words need to be spoke. She went to him, and he held her in his arms. Such strong arms and she nestled close to his chest, spooning her body into his, so that they became one. It did not take long for her to relax and fall asleep. He held her close and told her to rest. She did and she slept for hours! When she woke up, Jacorius was not there! She was covered and a pillow had been placed under her head.

She wondered was if it were all a dream, until she heard a noise from the kitchen. She got up and went into the kitchen and there he was cooking! Now this was her favorite pastime, to cook. So, Lashawn was happy to see that he was at home, in the kitchen. Jacorius completed her plate and brought it to the table, so that she could eat. He wanted her to take good care of the body that he planned to make his own one day! Lashawn did not know that he had wanted her so badly, but that was his plan, and he intended to get what he wanted! Lashawn had yet to tell Jacorius is that she was engaged to be married in 6 months! "Guess I will tell him soon. But not now!" Thought Lashawn to herself. "So, you can cook?" asked Lashawn smiling. as Jacorius sat her plates in front of her. "A little!" answered Jacorius. Lashawn is eating a wonderful breakfast. Lots of fruit, pancakes, eggs, grits, lots of meats. Sausage, link sausage, ham and bacon. She thought she would just eat and pass out again. However, Jacorius approached as she started to eat and begin to feed her. He touched her slightly in such a tender manner, as he fed her, that she didn't know if she was being consumed with desire from his touch or the sheer pleasure of enjoying the food! Jacorious brushed her cheeks, kiss their lips as he fed her strawberries dipped in whipped cream. Jacorius touched her thighs as he leaned in to put eggs in her mouth.

Whispering things in her ears, as she chewed. The things he said, sent shivers up her spine with anticipation. "Why do I see chill bumps on you?" asks Jacorius, in a low, deep, and seductive voice. Looking in her eyes, as he left her ears. "Uh-huh" answered Lashawn with the look of awe in her face, like "What the fuck!" "I'll tell you what. If you cold, let me heat you up! Have you eaten as much as you want?" asked Jacorius. With her eyes wide open and still chewing, Lashawn quickly nodded her head like a bobblehead doll! Slowly undoing the sexy Victoria's Secrets, see-through lingerie, Lashawn had on. Jacorius asked her could she lean back. He placed whipped cream and strawberries on her body, because as he put it, it was time to satisfy his appetite! He not only wanted the food, but he wanted her body! He touched every inch of her body with either his hands, tongue, or both! By the time he finishes, she thought she would lose her mind! He picked her up and went back to the living room and placed her on the floor. Dropping his boxers because that's all he had on. He lowered himself to meet her and they became as one. Satisfying all the hunger that had been built as they had eaten breakfast. They slept, after they were done.

Lashawn was at so much peace, but she knew that she had to come clean, and she did not know what Jacorius would do! She did not plan on losing him anytime soon. Jacorius was in his own world, as he drifted off to sleep, thinking about what else he could do, to ensure that Lashawn finally become his and only his! After about 2 hours, Jacorius woke up with Lashawn still in his arms. "Damn! she is looking so peaceful!" said Jacorius. "I got to constantly show her the affection, is what she's been needing and wanting. I got to make her mine! What else should I do to let her know I ain't playing?" said Jacorius to himself. Jacorius with the analytical and strategic mind he has, was laying there thinking all type of moves, to put on Lashawn. "I need to go smoke me a blunt of this Exotic weed and take a shower! I'll see this through! Yeah, that's what I'll do. I can't let Lashawn catch me though! Jacorius eased his arm off and under Lashawn's head, careful not to wake her. He put on his boxers, grabbed his Louis slippers, his phone, along with the weed and a cigar from his carry-on, and headed out the back door.

As he was rolling the blunt, he was checking his phone at the same time. They both hadn't really been paying attention to their phones, so he decided to check his. He had a lot of missed calls and texts! The only person he got back at was his mother. They talked for a minute. They had kind of resolved any problems they had. He knew his mother loved him, but it just seemed that she didn't have it in her, to fully have his back and that always bothered him! He almost texted Latonya back, but he was taking his mother's advice. "Feed her out of a long handle spoon!" Because Latonya was kind of throwed! "Damn! This is so unlike me. I have been tied up with Lashawn, for 2 days on some romantic shit! Ignoring my other women and money! Street money, not to forget checking on Dee-Dee and the strippers! I must be falling in love?! Who am I kidding! It's a wrap! I got to make her mine! Jacorius was analyzing the situation, as he smoked. If she will step out on this other cat, her situation, she'll step out on me! But then too, ole boy, isn't handling his business correctly with Lashawn.

I know how to do this! And that is be the man in which she is looking for. Let me go take a shower." Jacorius got through smoking, He went and took him a shower. As he was showering, he came up with a great idea! "I'm going to give her a sponge bath!" Jacorius got out of the shower, got himself together and found some brand-new sponges in Lashawn's closet. Found a nice size porcelain bowl, filled it with semi-hot water and body wash, enter the living room with intentions to please! "Great, Lashawn is still asleep." said Jacorius. He sat down next to her, softly pull the sheet back, and went to work. Lashawn was awakened by the feel of water touching her body. She slowly opens her eyes, as she felt she was in a dream. But the slow movements against her body felt so real! She became fully awakened, when she felt the soft touch on her breasts. She looked up into the Jacorius eyes and she realized he was giving her a sponge bath. He had started at her neck and was now on her breasts. But he assured her that he would wash every inch of her body to remove any remaining strawberry or cool whip, that had escaped his attention! The slow movements of his hands and the warmth of the water started a slow burn in the pit of her stomach. "Look, don't get heated! Because this is my way of pampering you. I don't want nothing in return." She couldn't help the desire that was building within her, and she knew she would want to become one with him again, before the end of the sponge bath. Now he was at her stomach, and she felt that she would lose it if he kept going! But he was insistent and told her that he would complete this task. Now he was at the juncture of her thighs, and she had to close her eyes to focus and not flip him over and take him!

She was trying to work with him, but the pressure was almost too much to handle. He saw her inner struggle and moved on to her thighs and down to her calf. Next were her feet. "Damn! I like your feet! They are so small and pretty!" Lashawn smiled. He finished his task and took Lashawn in his arms. "Baby, now I just want to hold you. Cool?" "Cool." said Lashawn, still smiling, eyes closed. Now, Lashawn had never been done like this before. Because every man had always started out holding her but quickly wanted more, so she prepared herself. After 10 minutes, she began to drift off to sleep, knowing that she would be awakening to Jacorius wanting more of her body. She awakened 2 hours later, still in his arms and he was fast asleep. Now, this was kind of surprising to Lashawn because, she just knew that he would wake up before her, wanting more of her. But at the same time, a part of her knew that Jacorius was deeper than sex with her. Oh, she knew that he was a street dude, a thug, who had gotten older and more mature. More of a playboy with money now! And plenty of women! His whole demeanor/aura screamed "I'm a dog!" But it was something about Jacorius she just loved! Her phone rung, interrupting her thoughts. Grabbing her phone and looking at the screen, it was her friend Cornelius, who she worked for at the law firm. "Oh, I got to answer this!" said Lashawn, as she got up, looking back at Jacorius while he slept. Not wanting to wake him, she walked toward the kitchen, as she answers the call. "Hey girl!" answers Lashawn. Cornelius sighs, letting out an air of relief. "Lashawn, girl you had me worried! Are you okay?" asks Cornelius. Giggling the whole time, Lashawn answered her and told her she just had to get away and chill. "Okay!" said Cornelius. "The next time you just pull a disappearing act, let me know! At least call in. You've been gone 2 days, and I haven't heard from you! Don't even answer the phone!" "I'm sorry!" said Lashawn. "It won't happen again, without you knowing first." "Must be a very relaxing retreat you're on!" Suspiciously said Cornelius.

"Yes!" stresses Lashawn. "You need me to come in today?" asks Lashawn. "No girl, go ahead and relax! Today is Friday anyway." "Thank you, Cornelius!" Lashawn and Cornelius talked for a few more seconds, before hanging up. As Lashawn headed back into the living room, she noticed Jacorius had gotten up and got dressed! Coming out of the bathroom with his phone up to his ear, leaning down kissing her. Now, her mind was in overdrive! Curiosity was sitting in heavy. Wondering where he was headed, and who he was talking to! She was afraid that Jacorius was about to leave, without returning. Since he has been with her 2 days, he might be tired of her, already! No. That can't be the case. Thought Lashawn to herself. "He has been treating me too good!" "Okay. Give me about an hour, I'm out of pocket." said Jacorius into the phone before hanging up. Not wanting to sound possessive or nothing but Lashawn had to settle her curiosity... "Going somewhere?" asked Lashawn, smiling at the same time. "Yeah. I need to run down to Daytona for a minute... To handle some business." said Jacorius. Putting a hand on her hip, with a sad smile. Lashawn nods her head. "Okay... I'm here." "What's wrong?" asks Jacorius as he hugged Lashawn and kissed her again. "Nothing." said Lashawn. "You think I'm not coming back. Don't you?" asks Jacorius. "I didn't say that!" "You didn't have to!" said Jacorius, still hugging Lashawn. "You want to stay up here this weekend?" asks Jacorius. "Well... I mean, yeah! But if you got something to do this weekend, don't worry about it, I'll be all right! I'm good." said Lashawn. Pulling his head out of Lashawn's hair and leaning back, looking at Lashawn. "I can't believe you said that!" said Jacorius. "You know I'm coming back up here today! You just stay put... Okay?" "Okay... I told you I'm not going anywhere... I'll be right here. You just be careful!" said Lashawn. "I will." said Jacorius as he got him a deep kiss from Lashawn and headed out the door. As Jacorius pulled off, Lashawn was leaning back against the door, relieved that Jacorius is coming back.

CHAPTER TWENTY-TWO

Chapter 18

LATER, THAT NIGHT, AND MORNING

Jacorius had done made his trek down to Daytona earlier that day. It was a Friday, money was flowing, and he had been missing in action, for the last two days. He had been neglecting his hustle. He really wanted to quit, while he was ahead of the game and get into some straight, legitimate hustles. He had stacked up enough money, to do other things. Along with the exotic entertainment management business. He had a place to live along with a couple of investment properties, he was straight! Actually, Lashawn was on his mind and what she had told him a while back. "I don't know what you're doing, but if it's not good, you need to quit!" Jacorius seen times he would have brushed what a woman told him about his business right off. But he really loved and cared for Lashawn and thought highly of her opinions and views. Besides, he wanted to be here with and for her in the flesh. Not from incarceration and definitely not from the grave! So, he was going to give some serious thought, to giving the hustle game up! Damn! I am really changing!" said Jacorius to his self, as he was headed back up to Flagler Beach. He had been talking to Lashawn off and on the whole day and to his satisfaction, she was still there! Waiting on him! Besides her going shopping online and talking on the phone, she had been there, patiently waiting on Jacorius return. Gerald had called to check on her, but he was more irritating than anything! It was 8:00 p.m. and she hadn't talked to Jacorius since 5:00 p.m. Now she was getting antsy! "I should just call or text him to see if he's coming back or what?" said to Lashawn. Grabbing her phone and speed dialed Jacorius. She let the phone ring five times before the voicemail came on. Lashawn almost left a message but decided against it. She didn't want Jacorius to notice the slight anticipation and anxiety in her voice. Because he almost picked up on everything with her! Kicking her feet up on the coffee table and setting her phone down, Lashawn just kicked back, wondering what was going on with Jacorius.

Stopping at a gas station right at right outside of Flagler Beach, Jacorius ran in the store to re-up on some cigars, Black and Milds, and a case of Coronas. This was going to be a long weekend! He had packed up some more clothes for the weekend, but he had forgot to get his other goodies, knowing Lashawn didn't like him smoking. In a hurry, Jacorius had left his phone in the car, missing Lashawn's call, and a couple of more calls. Once he got back in the car, he noticed he had three missed calls. Instead of returning the calls, he just turned his music up and pulled off! With nothing but getting back to Lashawn on his mind and hitting the highway, so he can go ahead and smoke a blunt he had rolled.

CHAPTER TWENTY-THREE

Chapter 18 (SPLIT)

Lashawn was still kicked back thinking and waiting. She was having a difficult time understanding what all was happening in her life. She was engaged to one man, but felt she was falling in love with another man! She had accepted the ring from Robert because she had truly felt that she was in love with him but as of late he had begun to take her love for granted. Lashawn had always made herself available to him, because she wanted their relationship to survive. She accomplishes her goal and was there for him, but now she began to wonder what Robert was giving her in return! She could never pick up the phone and call him and he immediately come. He came but he always had to work it out. Lashawn knew he would never just leave her stranded or at least she thought she knew. She had begun to second guess a lot of things, since Jacorius entered her life. She even wondered if Jacorius was too good to be true! Yes, Jacorius listens to her, was there for her but she wonders if and when he was going to change! Seems every man she met, changed and she was skeptical of Jacorius current behavior, remaining gone for a long period of time. Lashawn wondered, what would it hurt, to just get hers while it lasted and not worry about anything else! She was really contemplating living in the moment! But Lashawn knows that this would not be the case, because she loved hard! She was never a temporary person and what she got, she held on to hopefully forever! She never wanted a man to enter her life and lose him, at least not over anything small. She wanted a permanent and lasting love. Tired of her mind running so fast, Lashawn felt the need to relax. So, she went to take a bath, a long relaxing soak in the tub, should do her good. She ran the water and added bath salts, and green tea foam. She strips naked and emerged her body into the tub. "Ahh!" said Lashawn, as she leaned back and closed her eyes. Soon, she drifted off to sleep.

Jacorius had arrived at Lashawn's cave. Punch the code in at the gate and drove in. Grabbed his things and went inside. Once Jacorius was in the house, he sat his clothes down, went to the kitchen and put his beer in the refrigerator. He went back and put his cigars in his bags and went looking for Lashawn. "Lashawn!" said Jacorius as he walked through the house, looking for her. "Lashawn!" Jacorius called out. "She's probably in the bathroom" said Jacorius to himself. He went to the bathroom and tapped on the door. "Lashawn... I'm back." No answer. "Damn! I hope she okay. I'm going in!" said Jacorius, as he opens the door to the bathroom. And there she was, in the bathtub. "Lashawn! Are you okay?" asks Jacorius, approaching tub. "Oh, she sleeps". As Lashawn slept in the tub, her dreams went to Jacorius, because she felt so alive with him! He worked to please her, and it made her feel good! She went so far into her dream, that she actually felt like he's there with her caressing her body, making her come alive in every spot! Little did she know that Jacorius had entered the house and was going to talk to her, but as he heard her moan, he became fixated on her breasts as she breathed in and out. And on the way she kept licking her lips, ever so often.

When he couldn't take the sight of her anymore, without touching her, he reached out to awaken her. He gently touched her, but it did not awaken her, so he increased the pressure. Still nothing, as she was deep into whatever dream she was having, and it was having a direct effect on Jacorius! He wanted to be in the dream with her, but he wanted it to be his reality. Little did he know that he was in the dream! He stood and watched her erotic breathing, with his dick harder than Chinese arithmetic! When he could no longer take it, he called her name. "Lashawn." Her eyes fluttered open, but she was not immediately coherent to her surroundings. She thought, she was still in her dream and reached for him. However, she could not understand why he was dressed, because in her dream he had joined her in the oversized tub! Jacorius grabbed her hand, as she reached out to him. "Baby you alright?" asks Jacorius, as he held her hand caressing it. "Yeah, I'm alright!" giggles Lashawn. "Boy, I was dreaming about you!" "Oh yeah?" asks Jacorius. "Yeah... I was dreaming that you were in this tub with me!" said Lashawn, as she seductively lowered her eyes. "Well, we're about to make that come true." said Jacorius, as he releases Lashawn's hands as he smoothly took off his shirt, shoes, socks, pants, and boxers. In less than 30 seconds! Exposing his swollen and throbbing manhood and immediately stepped in the tub with Lashawn.

Lowering himself between Lashawn thighs, and which made him gasp, when she raised her thighs out of the soap suds and foam. Because that sight was so erotic looking to him, he almost erupted when she grabbed his tool, guiding it between her sugar walls. "Siss, shit girl!" said Jacorius, as he entered her core, and stroked up in Lashawn, causing her head to turn in ecstasy, with her eyes closed. Enjoying the pleasure and pain as Jacorius got his smash on in the tub. Wrapping her legs, tight around Jacorius's waist, like her life depends on it! Lashawn commenced to throwing it back at Jacorius, in a hard but very sensual way. Serving him! Rather they were serving each other. Jacorius slid Lashawn up a little, to where her back was up against the tub, exposing her breasts, so he can suck on them. He loved them, and he showed it, as he hungrily went at them with his mouth. Serving one breast as he caresses the other. He then switched up and served the other one!

The whole time she's pulling on his dreads and about to choke him with her legs! Throwing them around his neck and bucking wildly at his dick. A signal for him to get up in her belly! And that's exactly what he was doing...Getting up in her! By now, Jacorius was literally lifting her up out of the water, sitting her on the basin of the oversized tub, hooking his hands around her shoulders, as her legs were still around his neck, and fucked Lashawn like they were making a porno movie! "Ah, Ah, Oh, oh...Oh my god!" moaned Lashawn, as they aggressively got it on. By now, they were all the way out of the tub, against the wall, and sliding down the large countertop, towards the sink, knocking cosmetics on the floor! Now, Jacorius has snatched Lashawn off of the sink and is hopping around like Ving Rhames had that woman on Baby Boy! Lashawn is small, so with her legs still wrapped around his neck, it was rather easy for Jacorius, till he felt he was about to blast off! He made his way to the toilet stool and sat down. He kept Lashawn's legs up around his neck, and worked with her from that awkward position, till they both came, and they came hard at the same time! Both of them letting out animalistic grunts, letting their heads fall back, eyes rolling to the back of their heads. What a scene! They creamed each other! The nut was so good to Jacorius, he almost dropped Lashawn, but he caught her.

"Boy!" said Lashawn. Unwrapping her legs from Jacorius neck as he leaned back, and she hugged him around his neck, straddled him and start kissing him. "You almost dropped me!" "I apologize, but you almost choked the life out of me, with them lil strong legs! They both laughed and got back in the tub. Jacorius leaned back, as Lashawn sat between his legs. They were quiet for a moment, just relaxing. Jacorius grabbed a bath cloth and started bathing Lashawn tenderly and kissing on her neck and back at the same time. Occasionally whispering things in her ear, which is making her smile. Lashawn was on cloud 9! "Okay now! You keep that up and we'll be going at it again." said Lashawn. "Oh yea?" said Jacorius, as he placed the bath cloth between Lashawn's legs, cleaning her love box for her. After he felt like he had done enough, with the bath cloth, he used his middle finger, caressing the area surrounding her clit. Then he slowly moved to the clit, caressing it slowly, applying a little pressure, causing her to contract her PCG muscle, tightening her love around Jacorius's inserted finger. As he licked around her ears and caressed her left nipple, with his left hand. "Siss...oooh..wh-what are you doing? moaned Lashawn. "I'm trying my best to make you mines!" said Jacorius. All Lashawn could do is moan. She felt Jacorius getting back hard and that made her try to get up on it, so he can get it from the back. "Wait." said Jacorius, as he moved Lashawn to where her stomach was at the edge of the tub.

Arching her back, preparing to be entered from the rear, Lashawn reached back and grabbed and parted her butt cheek, Jacorius grabbed the other one, still caressing her clit, which was hard and throbbing now, he went down like a shark, and started licking her cunt, from behind! Now this caused Lashawn to inhale deeply out of shock and pleasure, because she was expecting to be penetrated from the back with Dick, instead it was tongue! Lashawn once told Jacorius that pussy eating was overrated but it seemed to him that she was enjoying herself! Going by her actions the way she squealed and moaned and almost jumping out of the tub. He stopped for a second, to spin her around, putting her legs in the buck, and he went down on her again! Underwater, sucking on her clit for a few seconds. He raises up for some air, and back down he goes again. As he was doing this, he simultaneously bites on her thighs. He repeated this for 5 or 6 minutes straight! Gently snatching her back in, as she tries to run. "Just stick it in...please!" screamed Lashawn. Jacorius was eating, licking, and sucking her up, driving her out of her mind. She didn't pay attention to Jacorius, when they first started, and he had sly way threw a Halls cough drop on the counter by the tub and discreetly grabbed it, while she was between his legs, and put it in his mouth.

So, she was feeling all kinds of sensations and catching chills. On the brink of tears, Lashawn begged Jacorius! "Could you please Fuck me? Please?" "Yeah." whispered Jacorius. "That's what I'm talking about." As he rose up and turned Lashawn over again, so he could hit it from the back...Again! He rode Lashawn like that a good while. By now, she had done cummed hard about 9- 10 times. He kept her from the back and slid back in the water till his back was against the tub and let her ride him in the reverse cowgirl style! Splashing water, until he came off. She immediately collapsed in his chest and he held her. "You wrong for that!" said Lashawn. "For what?" laughed Jacorius. Raising her head off of his chest, looking him in the eyes, and she smiles. "Nothing. Don't worry about it!" Jacorius had done freaked Lashawn, made love to Lashawn, and gangsta fucked her! He picked her up,and carried her to the bedroom and laid her down. He went and got two towels, dried her off and dried himself off and got in the bed with her, and held her. Within minutes, they both were sound asleep.

{Why does my body ignore, what my mind says? I try to keep intact, but now I'm in this bed.} "I know that's right!" said Lashawn, agreeing to Jill Scott's lyrics, in her song "I'm Scared", as it plays quietly on the radio. As she lays in bed with Jacorius, she watches him sleep, and plays with his chain. Fingering the diamonds in it. After a while, when Jacorius and Lashawn first started kicking it, this is the exact way she was feeling about him. Her mind was saying [No girl.. Hold it down, before you give in to him. You're engaged and plus you've never crossed that line before! Involvement with a street dude! But her body was saying: [Girl you need to go ahead and get you some of that!] Guess which side of her wins? But really, Jacorius met more than her physical needs. Everything else in which she was lacking, Jacorius fulfilled. He is just too good to be true! Let me get up and go cook for us.. For him! Jacorius awakens to the smell of food. "Damn! That smells good! I wonder what she's cooking?" Jacorius raises up out of the bed. He sits there for a minute, gathering his bearings, and he recognizes what is playing in the surround sounds: "It's been an hour, since you've been gone." "Damn! That's the old Jodeci, I'll cry for you tonight!" said Jacorius.

Then the thought hit him. "She must got our playlist of songs, in which made me think of her. He wanted her to make a playlist, so they can get together and listen and vibe to them. Some romantic shit! She didn't believe he had it in him. Jacorius got up and went to the bathroom, to get himself together. 5 minutes later, Lashawn came in looking for Jacorius. She noticed that he had got out of bed. "Oh, he in the bathroom!" said Lashawn, approaching the door. "You rather have waffles or pancakes?" "It don't matter! said Jacorius hollering over running water. "Yes it do! Which one?" said Lashawn, putting her hand on her hip, looking at the bathroom door. "Okay,waffles will be cool." "Alright." said Lashawn and she walked back to the kitchen. "Coming out of the bathroom, Jacorius grabs his phone and turn it on. He noticed he had some missed calls, texts, and voice messages. None of them really was important, so he only returned two calls and that was to his mother and his sister.They kicked it on the three way, as he put on some clothes to lounge around in, which consisted of his Louis Slippers, some linen shorts, and a tank top. Jacorius grabs his cigarillo, his weed, and a black and mild and headed out the back door, to Lashawn's patio.

Surprised, that Lashawn was right on his heels, clearing her throat! "Excuse me Mr and where are you going?" "Oh... Hey baby! said Jacorius as he turns around and gives Lashawn a quick kiss. "I'm headed out on your patio for a minute. You through cooking?" "Almost." said Lashawn, looking suspicously at Jacorius. "Who is that?" asked Jacorius's mother on the phone. "That's Lashawn." said Jacorius. "Man that lady sounds like she finna to get at you!" said Nicole, Jacorius's sister. "I know!" laughed Jacorius. "Who is that you telling my name to?" asked Lashawn. "My mama and sister." said Jacorius, as he stepped out and climbed the spiral steps to the patio, with Lashawn still behind him. "Oh, tell them heeey!" said Lashawn. "And you still didn't tell me, what you were bout to do out here." "Look at the ocean." answered Jacorius. "Here, holla at my folks." said Jacorius handing Lashawn his phone. "Oh you doing more than that Buddy!" said Lashawn before proceeding to talk to Jacorius's Mother and Sister. "Heey how ya'll doing?" Jacorius took advantage of this moment to quickly open up his cigarillo and roll his blunt up, with Lashawn eyeballing him, in surprise at the same time. "Uhh, uhh! I know you aint! Ya'll excuse me...Yo son, and Nicole, yo brother out here rolling weed in my face, and he knows i don't play that smoking stuff! I ought to knock it out of your hand!" said Lashawn, as she raised her hand like she was going to knock his blunt out of his hand. Jacorius just laughed and leaned away from Lashawn.

"Chill out Shawn. I tried to sneak away!" "What i tell you bout smoking though?" sincerely said Lashawn. "Baby i know." said Jacorius, still lighting his blunt up. Lashawn stood there watching Jacorius as he smoked, waving her hand, fanning the smoke. Jacorius got up and walked to the end of the deck, as she still scolded him, and talked to his mother and sister. "He coughing and still smoking that stuff!" "That's dat strong!" said Nicole, his sister. "Oh my God, tell me you don't!" said Lashawn. "Yes she do!" said Jacorius mother. "Yep." said Nicole. Her and Jacorius always been tight, so she's going to side with him mostly on everything. They talked for a few more minutes and Lashawn gave him the phone, and walked back in. "Oh...You got a call coming in from Latonya!" said Lashawn as she walked off, without looking back. Stunned, Jacorius watched Lashawn walked in the house. Jacorius looked at the phone, and for sure there was a call coming in from Latonya. He didn't answer it though, he continued to talk to his mother and sister for a few more seconds and hung up the phone, and finished smoking the blunt, and went in the house. Jacorius went and washed his hands, put on a dab of Blue- Chanel number 5, for men, and went to the kitchen. Lashawn was fixing there plates. "You want apple juice or orange juice?" asked Lashawn "Apple will be cool." said Jacorius. "You mad at me?" He walked up behind Lashawn, pressing himself up against Lashawn's behind. Moving her hair, as he kissed around her ears and neck, as she poured the juice. Of course this was turning her on, but she had to play it to the Tee! "What you think?" said Lashawn, as she slides out of Jacorius's clutches, and set the apple juice in front of Jacorius's plate. "I think you're mad, but not that mad. You're gonna tell me what for?" said Jacorius, with a sly grin on his face, approaching Lashawn again.

As she turned around, he was there! In her face, kissing her, reaching down and squeezing her round firm butt. The black boy shorts she had on, was really turning him on. She returned the kiss, for a brief second and slid away again. "Your food is getting cold.. Come on now.. You know what you did." I just don't like you smoking, that's all." What else was eating at her, was the call from Latonya coming in on his phone. "And who is Latonya? Aint that's the woman you said you wasn't messing with anymore?" said Lashawn. "I don't know why she's calling, but ain't no happening with me and her.. I'll assure you of that." Standing there with her hands, propped on her hips, blue and black flannel pajama top, unbuttoned, three buttons down, exposing her bra-less cleavage, was making Jacorius hot! "Okay." said Lashawn. She sat at the table to eat. "And why is you looking at me like that?" Said Lashawn, as she was spooning her grits. Biting his lips and smiling, Jacorius just shrugged his shoulders and started eating. He didn't want to seem, as if all he wanted to do was have sex with her, so he held his comment and started eating. Dick throbbing though! They were having fish and grits, egg omelettes, with sausage, bell peppers, onions, and cheese cooked in them and waffles. He loved her cooking. They ate and conversated, laughed a lot. Jacorius should have been a comedian! He was good at making people laugh. "Oh yeah.. I noticed all the music, that's been playing, is from the songs I gave you!" Said Jacorius. "Yeah! I didn't think you had noticed it." Said Lashawn. "All those fire ass songs! That make me think about you! You know I was going to notice." "So tell me...How do those songs, make you think about me?" Jacorius smiles and begin to tell her what she wanted to hear, but all of it was true! Jacorius was almost pouring his heart out to her. "See, a lot of those songs, I gave you, derived from me picturing you and I chilling, on a Saturday morning like this.. Listening to those songs, with you in my arms, in bed, just relaxing.

That's the vibe I was getting and wanting to make that fantasy come alive!..You feel me?" "Uhh,huh! I do!" Said Lashawn. smirking, with a sexy, dreamy look in her eyes. "Or like.. Tell me. How do you feel, and what kind of total recall/ vibe, feeling, or vision you get. Say.. When you hear Alexander O'Neal's, "If- you -were -here!" sings Jacorius. "If you were here tonight. What kind of nostalgic feeling you get?" "I don't know. You tell me." Said Lashawn, digging this conversation. She was smart, she knew exactly, what he was talking about. "Certain songs, conversation, reminisces, etc. A person can remember the smell, the vibe, or whatever was going on. That same feeling you had, comes over you. Well it makes me feel, exactly the way, I was feeling back then! Make me think about, laying back, with a woman, I'm feeling, on a late Saturday night. In the dark, with the only light shining, being the moonlight.. Matter of fact, making love, under the moonlight, while it's raining!" "You are a mess! So, what about a Saturday morning?" Asked Lashawn. "Some old Jodeci!" Said Jacorius. Lashawn sat there, for a minute smiling and suddenly snapped out of her trance and got up. "You through? Give me your plate." Lashawn grabbed Jacorius plate and headed to the sink, to wash dishes. Jacorius took this time, to blow him another blunt, and light his black and mild up.

As Lashawn was washing the dishes, she was thinking and smiling. Thinking about their conversation and picturing what Jacorius was talking about. Conveying, the good time feelings from the past to the present. Using that same energy, channeling that energy, to the now! To another person. "Hmmm.. Something to think about." Said Lashawn to herself. That's another thing she loved about Jacorius, his ability to have stimulating conversations, great imagination. Speaking of imagination, Jacorius was out on the patio, smoking some good kush, enhancing his imagination, plotting and planning his next move! He was thinking about one of their fantasy conversations from the past. "Yeah I'll do that!" Said Jacorius to himself. He was going to lay with her all weekend, might as well explore. After 10 minutes of standing out and staring across the ocean, Jacorius steps back in the house. As he walked in, he went to the kitchen, to find Lashawn, at the sink, still washing dishes. Those boy shorts was really turning him on! She felt his eyes, so she quickly turned around to catch him. "What?" Said Lashawn.

"Just looking." Said Jacorius, as he walked off, exposing a hard-on, through his linen shorts. He went in the living room, and sat down and turned on the TV, flipping through channels. Lashawn walks in, sits next to him, throws her thighs, across his and lean back against the armrest on the couch. "What are you watching? ESPN? What?.. Is it something wrong with my legs? You don't want them on you?" "No. They straight. Why you ask me all that?" Asks Jacorius, as he began to caress Lashawn's legs and thighs. "The way you was looking at them." Said Lashawn. Actually, Jacorius was thinking about making his fantasy conversation, he once had with Lashawn, come alive! The setting was just as it was in their fantasy! Talking about speaking something to existence! He had all day, so he wasn't going to rush it. Jacorius was serious about making Lashawn his, so he always made sure, he covered all bases, and continue to keep them covered. He kept in mind all of her needs and his duty to fulfill them.

True, Sex was one of them, but like Trey Songz said, Sex ain't better than love! And that's his aim with Lashawn. Jacorius and Lashawn's relationship, from the intro, was based on their ability to have need fulfilling conversations, and he plans to keep it up. Jacorius knew, most women fall in love with him, who have and will set aside time to exchange conversation and affection with them. They stay in love, with men who continue to meet those needs! Same thing it took to get her, is the same thing it takes to keep her! So, they sat there listening to some old Jodeci and talked for about an hour and a half or two, sitting in the same position. The only time they moved, is when Jacorius got up to use the restroom and when Lashawn got up to go and get them both a beer. At least three times! Jacorius made sure, that he was having caring conversations with Lashawn. Jacorius was so laced with the game, till it was a part of him, to the point of displaying qualities, like affection, attentiveness, warmth of personality, kindness, and tender sensitivity, came naturally.

Especially, when knowing the fact that, once these qualities, have been displayed in a relationship, it does more to arouse a woman, than any special technique, a man may have developed! But to Jacorius, this was no game, in the sense of being deceiving! No. He was dead serious! To him, it depends on the Mark / Target. If he is to use, what he knows as a tool of deceit, or just plain old good applied strategy, that's what game is to him. Tight strategy! Will he use it, to deceive Lashawn? Nope. Because, he wants to be with her, for real! "Excuse me!" Said Jacorius, as he was moving Lashawn's legs, out of his lap and getting up and going to the kitchen. Lashawn was watching him with curiosity in her eyes. When he didn't go down the hall, to the bathroom, on the strength they was drinking beer. "Where are you going?" Asks Lashawn. "Be cool!" Said Jacorius, looking back smiling. "What is he up to?" said Lashawn to herself.

Jacorius, had been spotted the bottle of Hershey's chocolate, earlier. So now, he was going to retrieve it, and make their fantasy come alive! He put it in the microwave for 30 or 45 seconds. Walking back to the living room, with his hand behind his back, smiling. Had Lashawn in suspense. "What are you hiding?" Asks Lashawn, as she was looking at Jacorius. "Walla!" said Jacorius, pulling the chocolate from around his back. "What you doing with that?" Asks Lashawn. Jacorius sat down next to Lashawn, in a way he can look her in the face. Because, she still was sitting with her back against the arm of the couch, legs on the couch. Leaning in, Jacorius gave Lashawn a sensual kiss. "You remember that fantasy?" Asks Jacorius. "Yes I do." answers Lashawn. Planting a tender kiss on Lashawn's lip, he unbuttons her flannel pajama top, at the same time and softly pinches the soft flesh, right below her navel. Jacorius brings the bottle of chocolate up to his lips and open the top with his teeth. Massaging Lashawn's right outer thigh, with his left hand, he lifts her thigh a little bit and poured a little chocolate on her upper thigh! Right where the shorts stop at. "Oh! What are you doing?" Asks Lashawn, as Jacorius quickly leans down and slowly licks and sucks the chocolate off of Lashawn's thigh. Then, he does the left thigh. "Man, what you doing?" Asks Lashawn, As she breathes hard and deeply. Jacorius was catching the chocolate, right as the warm liquid rolls deep into her inner thighs.

Couldn't take it any longer, he helped her out of her boy shorts and thongs. Jacorius was about to have fun with this now! He poured some more chocolate, at the top inner parts, so it can roll down, in the juncture of her thighs, towards the middle and he slowly but hungrily got it up with his mouth! Now, this was teasing Lashawn, out of her mind! He poured a little more, but this time he let some roll over her shaven split. And he leaned down and licked and sucked the sweet chocolate, out of her sweetness, making his mouth water, heavily and making her moan heavily! The stickiness of the chocolate, mixed with Lashawn juices, was making Jacorius get into animal mode! He poured some more on her upper thighs and her split again. By now, Lashawn has busted her legs open! Throwing one leg on top of the couch and the other one on Jacorius shoulder, as he got all of it up! Unable to take it anymore, Jacorius snatched his linen shorts and boxers off and went up in Lashawn and went to stroking! He had to stop after about the fourth stroke, because he was about to cum already! To delay that, he picks Lashawn up and took her to the bedroom, laid her down and went back in! The stickiness of the chocolate was doing something to both of them.. Making them both have an explosive orgasm. How they both were addicted to chocolate! Jacorius didn't stop, he got himself all the way back right, and kept on stroking! Lashawn and Jacorius went at it all morning, while all of their music they compiled, for a playlist played softly in the background. They finally slowed down a little, in the afternoon. They laid together, talked, listened to their music and elaborated on it, somewhat and slept. This was a great weekend for the both of them! All they did was enjoy each other and showed each other love and learned more about each other.

CHAPTER TWENTY-FOUR

Chapter 19

CAUGHT UP-3 WAY LOVE AFFAIR

After that weekend, on Flagler Beach, Jacorius and Lashawn have been seeing each other on a regular basis. Even though Lashawn was still engaged to Robert and still was living together but she spent more time with Jacorius, one way or the other! Either on the phone or they would meet up in the nearby city. Lashawn had even built her nerves up, to come to Jacorius's house. Jacorius knew, that she still was in her situation with Robert, but in his mind, he knew that she was on the verge of leaving him... At least that's what he was hoping. He had fallen in love and to his disbelief, he was ready to cross the line, and get married! Lashawn had fallen in love with Jacorius and he knew this. It just seems, as if she's caught between a rock and a hard place when making her decision to leave or stay. Jacorius hadn't made an ultimatum or proposed to Lashawn, as of yet, but his instincts was telling him, that she was stuck! In Jacorius mind, he feels like, if he just hold his feelings back down, he still could deal with Lashawn.You know, he be the N-I-G-G-A! And Robert can stay her man! But she might not get the same amount of time, from Jacorius in which she had got used to getting. The same amount of unconditional love? Yes. But the time factor would be altered. Jacorius didn't like the fact, of being the rebound guy.. Or so it seems. Seems like love, genuine love, will overshadow logic or what we think could be logic. Either way it goes, Jacorius mind is made up! He's going to try it! All or nothing with Lashawn, but keeping his patience intact. "Damn! I done cut off, all of my hoes!" said Jacorius to himself, as he sat on his leather couch smoking some granddaddy kush, looking through some photos. Him and the white woman, Janet remains friends, because she had showed him a new hustle. Legal, as a day trader, which had him good and paid, off of technology stocks. When he wanted to buy some real estate, or fly, high-end cars. Other than that, no dice!

No more freaking going on! Jacorius let Jan know, that he was heavily involved with someone now and was serious about making it work! When he told Jan this, she smiled at him for a couple of seconds and bursted out laughing! She said, "Jacorius, I wish you the best, but you and I both know that with a guy like you, that there isn't a bitch walking God's green earth, will make you faithful!" "I'll just have to make you out of a believer!" said Jacorius. Yeah Jacorius had changed, in the aspect of wanting to conquer a bad bitch, play the game, or just fucking every attractive woman he ran across. Although it was very hard, especially when he growed up being a dog and very promiscuous, addicted to pretty and fine women. Jacorius, has never ever in his 40 years of living consider being faithful! He could be in love with his main squeeze and still chase women! Now, Lashawn has came along. He feels guilty! cheating on her, even though she is still with a man!

That's what made him quickly fall weak, to Latonya's advances and this girl name Monesha, who he met at Famu's track. With both of these women they're hard to resist! Looking at their bodies and faces. Take Latonya for example. The weekend when she called Jacorius, as he was chilling with Lashawn on Flagler's Beach, when he didn't return her call, that made Latonya more ambitious as ever! Out of pride! That following wednesday night, Latonya popped up at Jacorius's pad! "Damn! I wonder who this is, coming here without calling?" Asks Jacorius, as he went to the door. Through the peep hole, he saw it was Latonya! Looking dead at the peep hole! "What the fuck!" Said Jacorius, as he opened the door. "What's up Latonya? You okay?" Yea Jacorius.. Well, not really! Look, I don't mean to barge in on you like this, can I come in?" Asks Latonya. "Sure!" Said Jacorius, stepping to the side, letting Latonya come in as he admires her outfit and shape at the same time! She had on a flimsy, short, light tan, with flower design, form fitting Vera Wang dress, which made her ass jiggle and shake, with each step. "Damn! Keep control! Jacorius. "What you said?" Asks Latonya, turning around quickly, to catch Jacorius watching her. "I was just thinking out loud. So what's up?" Asked Jacorius, trying to get to the point. "I can sit down can't I?" Asks Latonya. "Yeah, I ain't tripping!"

This is the price, Jacorius is paying, for being a great listener and a caring man on top of that! Latonya, is about to take advantage of that fact, even though, they're not together anymore. Latonya start telling him what was going on. The more intense her story got, the more intense Jacorius started listening. At first he was standing up, next he sat down on the couch next to her. Paying attention to the fact, that she had Jacorius on the hook, she turned things up, by crying! At first, she acted as if she was holding the tears back, then within seconds, the dam broke, and tears were everywhere! Including on Jacorious chest! She leaned into him, as he put his arms around her shoulder. "Everything is going to be cool." Said Jacorius in a comforting way. Thinking to himself, I wonder if these tears are real! She looked up into Jacorius's eyes, knowing that her eyes is what turn him on from the beginning! She gave him a friendly kiss on kiss on the side of his lips.

"Thanks! For being here for me." Said Latonya, as she massaged Jacorius's bare chest. "You cool." Said Jacorius, wanting her to get up, but at the same time, being nice. He would let her get herself together. "Okay now Latonya, get it together!" Said Jacorius, smoothly grabbing Latonya's hand, as she was making her way down to his stomach. "You know we got to chill out." Said Jacorius, trying to fight it. "I want you back Jacorius.. I need you!" Said, Latonya, as she forced her hand, down into Jacorius's pants and throwing her thigh across his thigh, allowing her warmth of her love box, to be felt by Jacorius, on his upper thigh. He could tell that she didn't have any panties on. "Hold it baby, you need to chill! Straight up!" Said Jacorius, but not really fighting her advances. Before he knew it, Latonya was kissing and biting on his stomach, with his tool, in her hand, stroking it and wrapping those big pretty lips around the head of it! "Damn Latonya! You need to chill." Said Jacorius. As the ecstasy of Latonya's mouth, was invading all defenses, he tried to put up. "Take me back baby!" Said Latonya, as she was giving Jacorius lip and mouth service and looking him in the eyes, at the same time. This made Jacorius, drop all pretenses of resisting, because now he was grabbing her by her hair and was thrusting his pelvic, upward in her mouth and before you knew it, Latonya is giving Jacorius the business! Riding Jacorius reverse cowgirl style. From the living room, to the bedroom, it was a wrap!

The next morning, Jacorius was feeling guilty, because all the time he was spending with Lashawn, he felt like she would know. But what quickly removes the guilt, is the thought of Lashawn, at home with Robert! Nothing never came of him and Latonya getting back together. Just fucking! Now this girl Monesha stepped into his life. Jacorius met her, when he was up at Tallahassee, on a scouting assignment over at FAMU. Jacorius hda been taking an online course, for sports management, through sports management worldwide. He took the 9 month certification course and graduated. After he graduated, he had to work up under there umbrella for 2 months. A training process. Jacorius was setting the stage, to exit out of the drug dealing game. The pills and exotic weed. A couple of days before the FAMU game, he had took a trip over to the campus and went to the sports complex. He was standing outside of the football players weight room when Monesha rode by in a white CLS 550 Mercedes Benz. That's the first thing made Jacorius look! A pretty woman, riding a foreign car.

They briefly made eye contact, but that was it. He thought he had seen her earlier, when he first pulled up on the campus. Jacorius was walking in the opposite direction, when he noticed that a guy came out to meet Monesha. He still didn't see how fine she was, because cars in the parking lot, was blocking his view and he wasn't really paying that much attention to her. Jacorius had walked around to the front of the building by the gym, talking on the phone, to a football player, a prospect, he was to meet with briefly. "Oh, you're coming out of the weight room right now?" "Yeah." Answers the football player. "Okay.. I'm coming in your direction." Said Jacorius. Mashing the end button and walking back towards the weight room. When Jacorius got back to the weight room, he noticed this fine redbone, with some dark blue tights and a white wife beater on and some long bushy hair, like Chaka Khan or Angie Stone. "Damn!" Said Jacorius. She was walking the track with a tall, slim dark skin dude. That's when Jacorius put two and two together. "Aww man! That's shawty who was in that Benze!" Said to himself. It seems like she felt him looking or heard what he was saying to himself, because, as she was walking the track, with the guy she met in the parking lot, she looked over at Jacorius. And he was Versace shades watching her! Once the football player, who Jacorius was there to meet came out, they greeted each other and walked back around to the front of the building and talked. About 30 minutes later, Jacorius was still in front of the sports complex when the white Mercedes rode through on a side street, coming from the track. "Damn that's her!" Said Jacorius, to the football player. "Do you know her?" The football player looked at her.

"Nope.. I'm afraid I don't, but she is looking mighty hard, like she know one of us!" "Yeah! That's why I asked you that!" Said Jacorius. All the time, Jacorius is sly way working his Mojo, by continue staring back at Monesha, but casually looks off, as if she don't matter for real! It seems like she didn't know which way to go, she was looking so hard. It was men working in the road, the way she wanted to turn, but they were in the lane, she was going to turn in. That lane was clear, but instead she went straight across the street, in the parking lot in which the president, and some of his top staff used. For a minute, it looked as if she was lost and the guy who had been walking the track with her, was on the passenger side, pointing, as if he was giving her directions. They turned around and came back out the way, they came in and turned right, past the workers and now they were slowly passing the building where Jacorius and the football player stood. Monesha was staring so hard now, Jacorius knew she was ready to choose up! Either him or his potential client. Instinctively, Jacorius smoothly opens his hands like, "What's up?" to Monesha. And she says to him: "I'll be right back!" As she was looking at Jacorius, smiling and talking to dude in the car, telling him that Jacorius looks familiar. "Might be my cousin." said Monesha. Now Jacorius didn't know who dude was or what. She might be playing it, mighty close with her man in the car, if it's her man! But one thing is for sure, she is ready to play! 10 minutes later, after Jacorius finished talking to the football player, he went to the park a lot to get in his car, which is a mint green S550 Mercedes Benz, sitting on some 24-in chrome rims. He prolonged long enough, to see was the girl, in the white Benze coming back. He wasn't into sweating a woman to long, like a stalker or something! Besides, she could have just been flirting and he had to go rent a hotel room anyway! As he was about to get into his car, he heard a horn blowing and low and behold it was Monesha! Into Floss mode, he left the door open to his Benze, so she can peek the Gucci interior, to show that he ain't bullshitting in life either! Turn up!

She pulled up, letting the window down. She quickly gave Jacorius a swag appraisal, with her eyes, and she got right at him! "What's your name?" "Jacorius. What's yours?" "Monesha." And they went from there. As they were talking, Jacorius mind went to Lashawn. He didn't know what it was, but when it came to other women and him getting involved with them, he always felt as if he's cheating! But he quickly would dismiss it, because she was with someone and go ahead and handle his business! As was the case with Monesha. They exchanged numbers and went from there. That night, he met Monesha at a restaurant. After they had dinner, they hit a laid-back club and had a few drinks, and there it went! Jacorius, buzzing on the alcohol, checking out the way Monesha is looking at him, when they talk, like she ready to eat him up! She loving his swagger, got him horny! Jacorius took Monesha straight to his room and fucked her good! Now that episode, started a series of Fuck Fests, from a distance. Monesha was from Tallahassee and Jacorius is from Daytona Beach. Started out as just cut friends, but Monesha wanted to get serious! Jacorius liked Monesha, but didn't have the capacity to love her. That space had been taken.

On the low Jacorius and Monesha, had been messing around for about two months straight! And on occasion, he still kicked it with Latonya! He tried to keep that to a minimal, especially when he found out, she was pregnant by her ex-boyfriend, Taiwan, and was supposed to get married to him soon! Let Taiwan be her man! Dee-Dee has started back coming around. Mainly business. When they met a couple of times a month, to square things up, with the exotic entertainment management and the opening of a strip club! He would let her seduce him, once, maybe twice out of that month, but most of his time was spent with Lashawn! Now after reminiscing about all his women and them tripping, because he done cut all of them off and calmed his fear of stepping over into the unknown boundaries. He jumped up, after he put the end of his granddaddy Kush blunt in the ashtray, grabbed his car keys and phone and called Lashawn and headed for the door. "It's time to go ahead and get my grown man on, and do what I'm supposed to do!"

CHAPTER TWENTY-FIVE

Chapter 20

Lashawn was out Christmas shopping, with her daughters, when she received the text from Jacorius. Saying that they needed to hook up later, if she could come, so they could talk. Jacorius needed to talk to Lashawn, to help her understand the love he had for her. He wanted to take care of her. He wanted to pamper her, but he was scared she wouldn't agree, to what he was about to ask! He know she was independent, but he wanted her to lean on him and let him take care of her every need! She had worked for so long, made ends meet for so many people, he knew she didn't know how, to slow down. But he had to try. He was scared, that her health was getting bad, since she barely slept and always complained of headaches! He knew he had to make her see, how much he needed her and would move mountains to help her with whatever! Lately she seemed to be distant and he didn't know why. So he was determined that night, he would get to the bottom of what was going on and let her know, what he planned to do to help. He went to the grocery store. He had some shopping to do. He got the steak, potatoes, onions and mushrooms. He still had to figure out, what vegetables to cook. Since he was undecided, he got broccoli to either steam or add to the salad. Next, he got her favorite ice cream, black walnut and some strawberries, just for a late night effect. He was heading to the checkout, when he saw the pink Tea-Roses. He knew she was not a flower woman, but he had just had to get them.

He would pull out a few stops. He arrived home, a couple of hours before their dinner date. He proceeded to grill the steaks and then he put the potatoes in the oven. He fixed the salad and placed it in the refrigerator. He poured the wine in the chiller. He places the flowers in a vase, in the middle of the table, to gauge her reaction, when she saw them! He knew she would know they were for her and wanted to see her facial expression the moment she saw them. He then put on some jazz and lit a few candles. Turning the lights down, he sat on the sofa, to think about the words he would use and say a few prayers! He needed her to be on board, with what he was about to propose. Lashawn was a few minutes early for the dinner date, but she couldn't wait to see what had Jacorius so worried, that he was about to cook her a full meal! Usually, he wants to go out. They always travel to an adjoining city, to see a movie and get something to eat, but he very seldom cooks. So, it must be something very important! She rang the doorbell and did not have to wait long. It was as if, he was standing there, waiting for her arrival. He pulled her into his arms and held her close and tight! She relaxed and felt the love surround her. She often still wondered, if this was too good to be true, but decided that right now, she would go with the flow. He moved back, just a little to look into her eyes and lowered his head, for a much-needed kiss. The kiss was short, because he was on a mission! When he pulled back and asked if she was hungry, she immediately smelled the food. Yes, she was hungry, starving to be exact! Jacorius escorted her, to the dining room.

The table was set, immediately Lashawn recognizes and admires his aim to please. "Hmmm, what you know about tea flowers?" Asks Lashawn, smiling as he pulled her chair out for her to sit down at the table. "I know a little something!" Said Jacorius, smiling at Lashawn's facial expression, when she seen the flowers. "Are they mine? Can I take them with me?" Said Lashawn. Stopping in his tracks, as he headed to the kitchen, to fix their plates. Jacorious turned around, with his mouth twisted up, with a "Girl stop it!" look on his face. "Aright, alright I know!" Said Lashawn. She knew the flowers were for her, she just had to ask. Lashawn was wondering, what was on Jacorius mind, she couldn't wait to hear it. He came back in the dining room, with a basket of soft butter rolls. Next, he came in with the salads! Then he came back with, the steak, potatoes, and mixed vegetables. "Wow! What are you trying to do to me? You trying to make me violate my work out!?" Asks Lashawn, as she picked up her knife and fork and began to cut into the steak! "No!" Laughs Jacorius.

"Just got to make sure you're straight! What I told you a long time ago?" "What?" Asks Lashawn. "That I'm going to take care of you! See about your every need." Lashawn pauses for a second, slowly chewing her food, looking in Jacorius eyes, smiling! Lashawn started back eating, before she answered. "Well?" Asks Jacorius. "I heard you... I remember you said that! Because, I recall saying something about, don't try to do it, from no salvation army!" "Yeah, because we had been talking about, that dude Calvin, who used to work with me! Move down here from Pensacola, going with Angela, who works at the college." Said Jacorius. "Yep!" Said Lashawn. "No baby! I told you back then, that I was ready! Or got the capabilities, to get ready!" Said Jacorius. "You sure?" Asks Lashawn, then she started giggling! "Straight up! I want to talk to you about that. Among some other things." Now, Lashawn is looking serious, because she was very interested, and curious about, what he was talking about! "Okay." said Lashawn.

"First of all, I want and need to know, what's on your mind? Why have you been acting so distant? Is it something I did? I mean... I've basically let go of every woman, I had deep relations and ties to, for what's on my mind, about you. Lashawn was somewhat stunned, but she knew that Jacorius wanted to make her his, exclusively! She knew that men like him, love to have more than one woman! A while back, she asked him was he a player, due to all the women on his Facebook page, giving him birthday wishes and saying all type of other stuff to him! But at the same time, she senses the loyalty in him and with her, it was all or Nothing! It was bad, because she hasn't even told him, that she was engaged to be married to Robert in the next month or so. "Are you going to tell me, what's really going on with you? Or shall I just go ahead and spill the beans to let you know, in full, what's really got me all amped up!" Continues Jacorius, snapping Lashawn out of her temporary gaze. Lashawn told him to go first. Thinking about it, for a couple of seconds, Jacorius realized that it was not the right time, at that moment! He was about to act out of sync. When he is more of a calculating and analytical person. "No, let's just eat and enjoy our meal first. You like it?" Asks Jacorius, smoothly resetting the stage and atmosphere. "Yeah... It's good!" Said Lashawn, as she smiles and lowering her eyes, at Jacorius, in an investigative way! "What Lashawn?" Laughed Jacorius, noticing how Lashawn is looking at him. "A mess!" Said Lashawn. They continued to eat, finishing the main course and salad. Once they were through, Jacorius took their plates to the kitchen, to be washed later and returned with two bowls, two spoons, and two different kinds of ice cream. "

"Okay... The black walnut is yours and the Moose Tracks is mine!" "Okay! You remembered." Said Lashawn. "Yea, I knew this was your favorite ice cream!" Jacorius sat down and talked with Lashawn on some basic stuff. Family, health, food, current issues in the world etc. After that, he took the ice cream bowls to be washed and returned and poured the chilled Merlot, in Lashawn's wine glass and filling his glass. Now it was time to get back down to business. "Now back to the issue at hand. You ready?" Asks Jacorius. bracing herself in her seat. "Okay...Shoot!" said Lashawn. "Okay... You know How I feel about you right?" "Right!" Said Lashawn. I need you to understand, exactly where I'm coming from, Lashawn... I done fell in love with you! I mean, I know you know, I love you, and I think the feeling is mutual... And..." "Jacorius, you know I love you!" Interrupted Lashawn. "Okay, okay, hold on." said Jacorius. "Okay. Go ahead." Said Lashawn, as she sipped her wine. Jacorius turned his up and downed it and poured another glass before he got started. "Anyway, like I said...I want to take care of your every need. You need to be pampered by me! I know that you always have been independent, but I'll take care of you financially, you can quit your job! I got you! Then, it seems like you be stressing too much baby! Don't get me wrong... I may be wrong! But I think, that's why you're sleeping has been thrown off and that's where the headaches come in at. A lack of sleep! So, I want you to just relax and let me love you and take care of you thoroughly. You just don't know how much I need you, Shawn! I don't know... I think I have... But I don't think I ever told you, how much I need you! But I'm telling you now! Woman I need you, just as much as I need my next breath like the R and B Nigga, Tank!"

Now, Lashawn was sitting their misty eyed and Jacorius continued. "Do you remember all those times, I'll be telling you that, I have something I got to tell you? But it's not the right time?" "Yeah!" Said Lashawn, as she wiped the tear, from falling down both cheeks. "Well, the time is now!" Said Jacorius "What I just told you, is part of it. Before I spill the rest of my guts, I need to know, what's been going on with you." Lashawn sat back and downed the rest of her wine and Jacorius was instantly giving her a refill. "Thank you." said Lashawn. "Go ahead finish Jacorius and I'm going to answer your question." Jacorius downed his drink and poured up another one, before he continues. "Okay. You know I've been wishing. I be wishing, that you would go ahead and leave your dude and get with me! Not just get with me, but with me for life!" Said Jacorius, as he rises from his seat, pulling the ring case out of his pocket and kneeling before Lashawn! Popping the case open, displaying the 5-carat diamond ring. "You told me, you were a long-term girl! So... I want you till death do us apart! Lashawn, will you marry me?" Jacorius had done up and did it! Turned his player card in! Lashawn had her hands up to her mouth, crying! Jacorious didn't know, were these tears of joy or what! But she was taking too long to answer. "Lashawn, are you okay?" Yeah, Jacorius I'm okay." He reached up and wiped some of Lashawn tears away with his thumbs. The others, he kissed them off of her face. Now she was smiling! Placing her hands in his hands. He kneeled back down. "Jacorious... I... I'm... Flattered!" "Don't be flattered, just say yes!" Said Jacorius. Jacorius, it's something I need to tell you." "Go ahead." "I... I'm engaged to marry Robert, next month!" Said Lashawn, and the tears went back to pouring.

Jacorious, stunned rose up off of his knees, slowly took his hands out of Lashawn's hands and walked off, running his hands through his dreads. "Damn!" Said Jacorius, as he walked through the house aimlessly. "Jacorius, Jacorius! Please come here!" "I'll be back. Just chill!" "Okay." said Lashawn. "I'll be here!' Jacorious walked out in the backyard, lighting a cigarette up, walking around aimlessly. "Nigga, you should have stuck to the script!" Said Jacorius, to himself. He was thinking about, how he had been giving his other women the cold shoulder. How he had been brushing them off! Latonya was pregnant now and wasn't sure, who the baby daddy was, between him and her off and on boyfriend Taiwan. When he denied that it was his, because he knew she had been getting back with Taiwan. That made her almost go ballistics! So, if he wanted to turn back to her, she probably would turn him down. Getting another woman wasn't the problem. Cause it was 20 to 1 ratio out here! What bothered Jacorius, was that he let his guards down! A collapse of his ego boundaries and he let his feelings got involved and did something, he said he would never do again! And that's falling in love, with a married woman again!

Well... Lashawn was almost married. He had to light a blunt up! As he stood there and smoked, Lashawn was in the back door watching him, as she wiped tears off of her face. She didn't know whether to leave or stay! She would ask him; did he want her to leave or what. She decided to wait, until he got through smoking. As Jacorius got high, he was thinking of his next move! Should he just go in there and tell her to get the fuck out? With Lashawn, he would be gentler. Should he just forget about it, swallow his pride and keep it like it is, and continue to fuck her? Should he move on and let Lashawn go on with her life? That was almost impossible! Because they were too connected. He couldn't and wouldn't look at her as a slut, but he almost did! But he kept his thoughts mature, by keeping in mind, how and why him and Lashawn was involved anyway. Robert was lacking, and he was macking! He remembers what an old nigga, out of Birmingham, Alabama told him once. 'To be a pimp, player, or a Mac man, you got to be cold as a snake, with the soul of a street walker!" "You got the soul of a street walker! The drive to get money, but you ain't quite got the heart and coldness of a snake. Which don't care about nobody! You care too much for real. But when you get the coldness down packed, the world can look out!"

So, was he macking and had fallen in love? "Nope. I was trying to make her my main squeeze!" Said Jacorius, trying to compensate and make excuses for him crossing the line, knowing he's supposed to keep it, "Money over bitches!" In slight resignation, Jacorius dropped his head in defeat. He hit the last of the blunt and threw it down, and that's when Lashawn stepped out of the door, cautiously walking up behind Jacorius and touching him on the shoulders, startling him out of his thoughts. "Oops my bad!" Said, Lashawn as she jumps back, reacting to Jacorius sudden movement. "No, you are straight." Said Jacorius, as he stood there, looking at Lashawn. Reading her, deciding which way to go. "Keep it player, and don't trip!" Jacorius thought to himself. "So, what's up?" Asks Jacorius. "Jacorius, I'm sorry!" Solemnly said Lashawn. "Why didn't you tell me?" Asked Jacorius, careful not to get emotional. I over E, intellect over emotion! "Well... I was... I didn't know how to tell you, well I did... But before I knew it, you had done got in my spirit, up under my skin! You want to know what's been wrong with me? Well, that's it! I have fallen, so in love with you, and I'm knowing that I'm supposed to be getting married soon! It has me in my mind just..." Lashawn threw up her hands, in surrender! "I don't know Jacorius!' and fell into his chest. He almost hugged her, and comforted her, but he barely touched her arm and to her surprise, he wasn't hugging her! Now she was confused and hurt! She knew she had hurt him, but she didn't think he would leave her hanging! "Lashawn." "Yeah." answered Lashaun, as she looked up in Jacorius red eyes. "What's it going to be?" "Huh?" "You heard me!" Said Jacorius, in a dangerously quiet tone, in which kind of spooked Lashawn! "Jacorius... I don't know! Let me do some thinking about this, before January roll around. I promise..."

"Get the fuck out of my house!" Quietly interrupted Jacorius. "What?" Asks Lashawn, kind of lost. Clearly Jacorius was mad. "Get the fuck out!' said Jacorius, in a harsher tone. Lashawn was hurt. She never has seen Jacorius mad with her. But she did what he said. She looked at him a second and walked back in the house, grabbed her purse and left! 'Damn! Why did I do that?" Jacorius asks his self, after Lashawn left. He should have handled it better than that. He had got mad. He felt hurt! Because he felt played. He actually, played his self! So much for I over E.

CHAPTER TWENTY-SIX

Chapter 21

THE AFTERMATH

3 weeks had passed, since that disappointing night, at Jacorius's house. He laid around every night, reminiscing about conversations, with Lashawn, being with Lashawn, everything about Lashawn! It wasn't like they couldn't reach each other. She had been texting him, apologizing and telling him how much she loved him and what he meant to her. She even sent some scriptures! Jacoruis read every one of her texts, but didn't answer them. Jacorius kept himself busy, hustling and preparing for the opening, of his new strip club! Getting to the money! Is how he always dealt with recovering from a fall. A hustler's way! Jacorius had got this old warehouse and now had a crew out there cleaning and remodeling. Building a stage or two, a couple of bars, and a big ass VIP section. He was going to try his best to make the club be like the king of diamonds! In Miami. Jacorius had not really been messing around, with none of his old flames, with the exception of Monesha, and Dee-Dee.

Yeah, he called Dee-Dee up for old times' sake. He loved how soft her lips were and how she worked with the sour apple flavored, motion lotion! Dee-Dee introduced him to a Dominican stripper who looked like Joe Budden's ex-wife Tahiry. She was all the way down, for a threesome! So, he was getting it in with her and Dee-Dee kind of frequently! He had taken a couple of road trips, with the strippers, just like old times, hitting different clubs, across the U.S. back to living fast! But, whenever he returned home, alone, he would lay back and think about Lashawn! Wondering how she was doing and what she was doing. He would lay back and listen to the playlist they had done made. All of the songs had him thinking hard! But Alexander O'Neal's classic, "If you were here Tonight" always had him missing Lashawn... Badly! He would lay there and just stare at the ceiling, with tears of frustration in his eyes.

It was getting closer and closer to Lashawn and Robert's wedding. Her and her friend were going to have a double wedding, and it was close to the time she had her book club, black and white ball! She wasn't even excited about neither one. Well, a little excited about the ball, but not the wedding. Robert was proving himself unworthy by the days! He was supposed to always have her back, and he didn't! Not to mention, that she knew about his affair with his high school sweetheart! On the other hand, Jacorius always had her back. She couldn't understand why he wouldn't answer her text or calls! Well, she knew he was mad and hurt, but the relationship they had, should supersede all hurt. She remembers once, when her and Jacorius was talking about fighting for a relationship, after maybe she wants to end it, and Jacorius had said he probably would try to get things back straight once. But after that, no ass kissing! "You wouldn't even try to fight?" Lashawn had asked him. "Maybe a little... But nope... No ass kissing! Would you want me to fight?" Jacorius had asked. "Yeah!"

answered Lashawn. But now that, that time has come to fight, Jacorius didn't put up a fight, and that hurt Lashawn also. "Who am I going to talk to now?" Lashawn asked herself. Robert had been asking why she had been acting so funny. As long as he had done been with her, he should know! He didn't really seem caring. She didn't really know if she would go along with the wedding! Ever since that night Jacorius proposed to her, she been going through it! Her same routine, remain the same. She would get out of the bed at night and go to the den, play on the computer, except now she would always put in her earbuds and listen to some of her and Jacorius Playlist, reminisce, and cry!

Jacorius woke up one particular morning, grabbing his phone, wanting a text from Lashawn. He missed her so much! Turning his phone on and to his delight, there was a text from Lashawn! A three-part text. She was really pouring it on heavy, because Jacorius laid back and smiled to himself. Contemplating on hitting her back up! Once he read the text two times, he was about to check more messages. He notices, he had a voice message from Lashawn. He listened to it. {Hey Jacorius. I know you must hate me now... I know I hurt you.. And I am woman enough to say, I was wrong !But if you really loved me, like you say you did... You would forgive me! Now, I usually don't do this, but I know I was wrong. OH, do you hear what is playing in the background?} She had Jill Scott' song {So gone (what my mind says)} playing. That's what I was going through with you. And still am." A long pause. "I don't know, I still haven't decided on what I'm going to do. I wish you would talk to me! But if you don't want to, I understand... But know that, I will always love you, no matter what! And I will always have your back! Bye.} She ended the voice message, and Jacorius was laying there thinking. "Fuck it!" Said Jacorius and texted her back. {I still love you. And still got your back!}

When Lashawn receives the text, she smiled, and text him right back! {Nice to know! Friends for life?} For a minute, Jacorius was thinking, Lashawn was trying to play him, for a sucker or something! Then he thought about it, that's just how she kicks it. "Fuck it! I'll text her back." After about 3 minutes, Jacorius text her back, {Yeah.} And that was it. Now this almost made Lashawn mad, but she calms down. "At least he texts me back and is communicating with me." Jacorius had been thinking about doing some sheisty shit toward Lashawn! Like fucking one of her partners. Or just go ahead and fuck Tanithia. Tanithia was Felicia's niece by marriage, who used to have lunch with them at Henrietta's, and she was all on Jacorius dick! Since she thought that she knew, what was going on with Lashawn and him. That made her turn up! A couple of times, when Jacorius had gone to Henrietta's, to kick it with Lashawn, Tanithia and Felicia was there, and having lunch with Lashawn. Tanithia seems, as if she went into a zone! She would be winking her eyes at Jacorius on the low.

Blowing kisses! Even went as far as busting her legs open at Jacorius! At first, he thought it was a game they were running. So, he told Lashawn, to see what she says and check her reaction! Lashawn's only reply was, "I told you she wants you... Bad!" And started telling him all type of stuff about to Tanethia. Jacorius seen times he would've went ahead and Fucked Tanethia! But he was feeling Lashawn too much. "See how loyal I am to you? I kept my dick up out of Tanithia!" Jacorius once told her. So now he was thinking about all that. "She good people though. I hope she haven't been fooling me." Said Jacorius. "Damn. She still ain't talking right.. I don't know! I'll probably keep things as it is, just play her from a distance. I don't know!"

A week before the wedding, Lashawn and her friend Janetta, was going over rehearsals and arrangements at the church, they were having the double wedding at. Lashawn was great at putting a mask on, but at this moment, it's written all over her face! "It'll be best, if we have the photographer stand here and take pictures during the... Girl what is wrong with you?!" Asks Janetta, snapping Lashawn to attention. "Oh, my bad Janetta!" Laughs Lashawn, putting her hand on her chest, as if someone scared her. "Are you okay? You got butterflies or something? You've been out of it!" "I got a lot on my mind. I don't know! It's just... I'm not excited, like I supposed to be." "Don't tell me you got cold feet now?" Said Janetta. "No... It's not that... It's... I don't know! It's hard to explain." All the time, she was thinking about Jacorius! He had a right to be mad. "But don't do me like this!' Thought Lashawn to herself. It had been a couple of days, since Jacorius responded to her text. And that made her happy. But now he is acting funny! She had the good mind, to go over to his house and give him the business!

Make him feel her! Then how would that look? When she's about to get married! Now she's feeling like she doesn't want to get married, not to Robert. It wasn't in her heart anymore. "Well try me, Lashawn! Explain it to me. I might can help. Said Jenetta. Lashawn gave Jenetta an under-eyed look for a couple of seconds and smiled. "You think so?!" "Try me, Lashawn!" "Okay! Have you ever done something, was supposed to be right, but feel so wrong, and in turn did something, what may be wrong or wrong in the eyes of others? That felt so right to you?" "Nope!' answered Jenetta. "Come on Nett! I know you have!" Said Lashawn. "Well, maybe once or twice, I don't know! You want to tell me what's going on with you Shawn?" "Not right now." Jenetta looked at Lashawn for a couple of seconds. "Is that bad?" Asks Jenetta. "No... Well, it all depends, on what you call bad." Said Lashawn. "Cut the BS Lashawn, we girls you can... OOO!" Said Jenetta, putting her hands up to her mouth.

"Lashawn, you been cheating!" "No! Look, before you jump to conclusions, or start spreading some type of rumors, it's like this, who's supposed to have my back. Faithfully. Don't have my back! And who would have my back or do have my back, circumstances are hindering, happiness for me! You understand that?" Asks Lashawn, in a serious tone. "I'm sorry Lashawn! But whatever it is girl, please just follow your heart." Said Jenetta. "I hear you. But look, I got some things to do. I'll get with you later!" Said Lashawn, as she grabs her purse. "But... But... What about this rehearsal? You can't just leave like that Lashawn! Said Jenetta to Lashawn's back. "Watch me!" Said Lashawn, as she headed out the door. Lashawn got to her car and crunk it up and took off! To where she was headed, she did it even though! She was just riding, as the tears flowed down her face. "What am I going to do?" Lashawn asks herself. She was feeling like Latoya Luckett, torn between the two!

Jacorius was at his new club, watching the workers do their thing. He was excited about the grand opening, which was coming soon. He already had flyers out and advertisement on the internet, Facebook and all! Dee-Dee and himself had a whole lot of strippers lined up to work there. His aunt had flown down from Atlanta, she was going to run the kitchen part for him. Everything was set! He even had "2 Chains" booked to come to a show! His career with the sports management thing, was slowly getting off the ground. The exotic entertainment management is still bubbling heavy! Real estate and buying and selling stocks, ETF's, Crypto currency, and mutual funds, had him eating good! He was about to make a successful exit out of the hustle game and clean his money up! The only thing is missing, is the wifey! Lashawn! "She about to marry this other cat! "Oh well." Said Jacorius to himself. He had about gotten over the hurt, it's just that he would dwell on things, a little too much. Jacorious checked on everybody, to make sure they were straight before he left.

Afterwards, he went and hopped in his new Cadillac XTS in left. Where was he going? He didn't even know! Just was riding and thinking. And smoking weed! Truly Jacorius was stressing on the low. With everything going good for him, he still felt incomplete. He had on some nice old school slow jams. When Karen White and Baby Face's old school classic, "Love Saw It" came on, he really was zoned out then! He almost grabbed his phone and called Lashawn. He was thinking about it hard! Then, the straw that broke the camel's back is when the radio started playing "Musiq Soulchild's", "My mind gone half crazy, but I can't leave you alone!" "Damn!' Said Jacorius grabbing his phone. "Fuck it! I got a call her."

Lashawn was riding up 95, heading to Flagler Beach, when her phone wrong. She really didn't want to be bothered, she was trying to work things out in her mind, so she just let it ring, without even looking at the caller ID.

"Damn! She doesn't want to answer the phone!" Said Jacorius. So instead of leaving her a voicemail, he texts her a simple message: {I need you!} And hit send. He waited for the outcome. It was strange, but he ended up in Flagler, at this park, where him and Lashawn had met up at before. He got out of the car, just as it started to rain and headed to the gazebo. "Maybe, I shouldn't have even called her or text! Look like I'm chasing her now!"

Lashawn was riding around in the rain in Flagler, aimlessly, and mind still running, when she decided to check her phone, to see who had called and text. "Shit! I missed his call and text!" Said Lashawn to herself. She opened the text and read it: {I need you!} Trying her best not to text and drive, she pulled to the first parking lot, she rode up on and text him back: {I need you too! Where are you?}

Jacorius was chilling up under the gazebo, when Lashawn's text came through: {I need you too! Where are you?} Jacorius texts

Lashawn back, letting her know where he was at: {At this park, up under a gazebo, ducking the rain. In Flagler!] "I know she's going to trip, think that I'm tripping, when she gets this text." Said Jacorius and indeed she did.

"What!?" Said Lashawn, when she got the text. She was surprised and delighted! "I wonder what he is doing up here. I am not going to ask him." She already knew, what park he was talking about. Because they had been there together before. {What a coincidence. I'm in Flagler too! Will be there in a second.} After she sent the text, she was on her way! And another coincidence was that Mary J Blige's "Mr. Wrong" was playing in her car! Again! "You called and I run."

"Oh my God! She up here!" said Jacorius. He texts her back. {Bet!}
"I wonder how this is going to go?" Jacorius asked himself. About 5
minutes later Lashawn was pulling up. For a second, she was hesitant
about getting out in the rain, until she seen him, walk from under the
gazebo. She jumped out of her car, headed up the sidewalk; to go to
him and he was also headed towards her, to meet her... In the rain!
Once they met up, it was like something off of a movie! Undistracted
by the rain, they hugged and kissed! Letting their love and passion
take over. "Jacorius, I'm sorry!" Said Lashawn as she cried. "You cool
baby. Let's get out of this rain." Said Jacorius as he wrapped his arms
around her neck and walking her to the gazebo, to shelter her from the
rain. Once they got under the gazebo, he held her in his arms, as she
cried in his chest. "I'm still confused!" Said Lashawn. "I know!" Replied
Jacorius, as he smooths Lashawn's hair. He wiped her tears away and
gave her a kiss. She smiled and hugged him tighter. "Everything going
to be all right." Said Jacorius. "I needed this! Thank you for being here
for me!" Said Lashawn.

"Now, tell me why you are up here?" "To be honest Shawn, you were on my mind! You been on my mind every day, matter of fact! Anyway... I left my club, and..." "You got a club now?" Asks Lashawn. "Yeah... Working on it! I'll tell you about it, anyway I left the club, riding, listening to some music and something led me up here... To this park! Reminiscing, I had already called you, before I got here. You didn't answer... That's when I text you, and I meant what I said in the text!" "I know!" Said Lashawn. "And I need you too! I'm just so confused right now." Jacorius just looked at Lashawn and wraps her back in his arms. After a couple of minutes of silence, Jacorius just had to know, why was she up here! "You'll never believe what happened!" Said Lashawn. She started telling him about the rehearsal at the church, the conversation her and Jenetta was having and how she up and left the church! Riding, thinking, thinking about him and just came up to Flagler! "Divine intervention?" Asks Jacorius. Lashawn leans back and look at Jacorius, smiling. "I don't know! Might be. Look let's get out of this weather! I can't get sick!" "Where are we going?" asks Jacorius. "Where do you think? To my cave!" said Lashawn. Jacorius smiled. "That's what's up!" It still was raining, so Jacorius tried his best to shield him and Lashawn from the rain, with his jacket and walked back to her car, opens her door for her, and went to his car and followed her to Flagler Beach.

CHAPTER TWENTY-SEVEN

Chapter 22

ROBERT THE FIANCÉ

That night, at Lashawn's cave, they made sweet tender love and just laid in each other arms! Soaking up one another's love. When the subject of Lashawn's wedding came up, she still didn't know what she was going to do. Because now, it wouldn't be right to go on through with Marrying Robert. When she's crossed a line, in which took her already, doubtful, love, mind and heart, in what she had tied in with Robert to another breed of man! A street nigga/ convict, a hustler, a thug, a gangster! If her friends and family knew what was going on, they would disapprove! They would scream like Mary J Blige said her family screamed, on "Mr. Wrong!" Mary don't do it! No, Mary! And Lashawn's like, "I guess they never had none!" Her and Jacorius got along so well, versus her and Robert, not getting along so well. She tried! She has gotten tired of saying the same old thing and Robert's not hearing her! But, Jacorius, he does. Didn't he once say, it's a cry that he only hears? Her only thing with him is, will he be around! He's not all the way, 10 toes down in the streets, like a young buck, but he's heavily involved! Not to mention a stable of women! Versus Robert, a college grad, an engineer, a working man. A security move, not to mention, they've been together a while! But he's in an affair. Bad boys ain't no good, good boys ain't no fun!

This explains, to a certain degree, Lashawn's reoccurring fantasy of a bad boy! Since she was 17 or 18. She understands now or is it like Jacorius keeps stressing. His favorite saying, Divine intervention! It could be. Is what her faithful mind is saying. Lashawn was raised in the church, like the average black woman, in the south. So, her gravitation toward God, or ideals of her Baptist upbringing, makes her receptiveness, keener, than the average black woman, who is not raised in the faith. It could be a game, coming from Jacorius! But she is willing to grasp, the notion of divine intervention, in her relationship and life! Due to the events and things, she's been going through lately and how some things, people and events, intertwine in her life for the good or bad, makes her think about somethings prior to what's going on now with her. She remembers once, Jacorius asking her about, what prayers that she can remember, making, dealing with her life and if the manifestations, of what she asked for, is coming to pass.

Her answer was "Yeah! A friend and would he send someone to pray with me!" Jacorius told her about a prayer he had made a couple of years prior to them meeting and after them meeting, how long it had taken for them, to actually get closer and all the things they went through together! So, all of this was on Lashawn's mind now. Full blast! Driving home from Flagler's Beach, Lashawn was contemplating on calling Robert and telling him the wedding is off! Matter of fact, they were through dealing! Thinking, why she's listening to one of her and Jacorius's playlist. Angela Winbush's "Angel" was on. Jacorius had told her, that he had found his angel, and wanted that song, on one of their playlists. Listening to the words, she was thinking that he was her angel! "A couple of days now. I got to barbecue or mildew!" said Lashawn to herself. "Ugh! What am I going to do?!"

Driving back through Daytona, Jacorius was back in deep thought. "I don't know if she's going through with it or not, fuck it! I don't care! All of these women out here, and I can get more than one!" said Jacorius to the empty car. He was listening to one of his and Lashawn's playlist and "Surface" old school song came on. "Only you can make me happy!" And his mind went to Lashawn and the exclusivity of their relationship. He wants her to his self! Well, time will tell. He headed straight to his club, to see their progress. Lashawn was supposed to meet him over there, to check it out! So, he called her to see was she still coming. No answer! So, he left her a message. {Just checking to see, if you're still coming through... Love you!} "Damn, I wonder what she is doing." Said Jacorius, looking at his phone. He didn't know, at this time what Lashawn was going through.

CHAPTER TWENTY-EIGHT

Chapter 22 (SPLIT)

When Lashawn got the call from Jacorius, she had a little drama going on. Lashawn had gone to Henrietta's, when she got back to Daytona, to make sure everything was okay. After that, she went over to the office for a minute, to go over some work. Afterwords, she went home. She got out of the car, put her key in the door and went in and was met by Robert. "You scared me!" Said Lashawn as she exhales the breath she just quickly inhaled, from being startled. "You are going somewhere?" Asked Lashawn. "No!" Said Robert. "Where have you been Lashawn?" 'Where have I been?" Repeating the question, with attitude while placing her hands on her hips. "Yeah! Where were you last night?!" "I took a trip up to Flagler... To get away! All this pressure and..." "What pressure Lashawn!?" Interrupted Robert. Look... All these questions... When did we start doing that!? Ask Lashawn. "Check it out Lashawn. You are about to be my wife baby. It's time we start..." "Start what?" Interrupts Lashawn. "Start reinforcing my suspicion of you and your activities?"

Rolling his eyes and putting his hand up in a hold up manner, Robert was going to nip this in the bud! At least that's what he thought. "Don't start that shit again! Lashawn you..." "No, don't you start your shit again! You know I've been quit asking you, where have you been! Or why do you got to walk out of the room, when your phone rings!" "I don't have to stand here and just listen to this... I'm about to leave, and when I come back..." "See, that's your problem Robert! You won't..." "What's my problem Lashawn?" Interrupts Robert. "You won't listen!" Screamed Lashawn, On the borderline of tears. "I keep telling you the same thing, over and over. But you're not hearing me!" Robert stood there, half stunned and half sympathetic. He turned around and walked towards Lashawn. Stopping with an inch from her... He reaches and grabs Lashawn by the shoulders and attempted to hold her. Lashawn removes Robert's hands from her. "Lashawn, what's wrong?" She stood there crying, shaking her head. "Is it the wedding?" Asks Robert. Looking at Robert in disbelief. You haven't been hearing me." "Hearing what? Talk to me Lashawn!" Said Robert, as he goes ahead and hug Lashawn, slightly against her will. She resists for a couple of seconds, but she gives in. Allowing Robert to console and caress her. Something he was lacking in.

His sensitivity towards Lashawn. Robert led her to the bedroom and sat down with Lashawn and held her. After her tears subsided, Robert begins to try and get to the bottom of things. "Lashawn baby, tell me what's wrong. We're about to be married. We don't need to go into this, mad at each other all the time!" "Look.. It's like this.. I need you to listen to me. I need to know that you really got my back! At times, you been making me feel like... You really don't care, if this works or not!" "Lashawn. I've been so busy, at the office... You know what my job consists of!" "Oh, like my job and the things I do, don't keep me busy?" Asks Lashawn. "Yeah! They do keep you busy, Lashawn. But... Just believe in me! We're going to work it out!" Said Robert as he planted gentle Kisses on Lashawn. "Now finish telling me, what's bothering you. I want to get to the bottom of this, now!" Lashawn didn't know whether Robert was being sincere, with this reflection of affection, he is displaying or is it his famous way of making up? Being sweet, which makes her madder! Lashawn let the floodgates down and let him have it!

She was reminding him of what he already supposed to know! Her needs! She held back some things though, yet gave him the basics She was feeling like, she had to brace yourself! Because, if Robert was sincere about how he was going to be more affectionate, caring and truly have her back, she wouldn't worry about him wanting sex in exchange of him listening to her! But if he proved her right, then she was on point with bracing herself, because he wants his payment! Sex! Lashawn was right. After his caressing and gentle kisses, he was aiming to arouse her sexually now! If Robert knew his woman, or just women in general, he would know that a woman is usually aroused when she chooses to be aroused! Without the environment of affection, the sexual event is not predictably pleasant for the woman unless, she just trying to get her rocks off! She has had some pleasant moments with Robert, but as of late the affection was missing! So now, sex with Robert was mere duty, or an act! She hasn't had sex with Robert since June 29th and now it's January! And not to mention that she told him: "If and when I have sex with you again, you're going to have to use a rubber!"

That offended him, knowing that they were engaged to be married soon. Robert's hands had made it down around Lashawn's ass. "Time to pay up!" Is what Robert's action is saying. Lashawn engaged in a moment of a kiss with Robert for a second or two and pulled away! "Why does it feel like I'm paying you, with sex, every time I need you for something? Such as listening to me." Asked Lashawn. "Come on now Lashawn!" Said an exasperated Robert. As he continued to make his advances. "Everything, I have done, that you don't like... I want to make it up to you. I'm going to be more, affectionate. I'm going to spend more time with you." Said Robert, as he continued making his advances. Lashawn mind was in turmoil right now. She wanted to believe Robert, but his present actions are putting him back in the same category he was in, in her mind anyway! Then a feeling of guilt came over her. Her newfound loyalty she shared with Jacorius, had her wanting to stop Robert's advances, right then! Matter of fact, had her wanting to just leave, right then, and find Jacorius! She knew that he was expecting her, to be on her way to his club! Right then, the connection that her and Jacorius had her thinking, that he would know what her and Robert were close to doing. Her mind was flashing, to the times her and Jacorius was at that very heated moment, she's at right now! As she was caught up in her daze, Robert had done undressed, and was undressing her, as tears flowed freely down her face. "Lashawn If it makes you happy, I'm going to use a rubber." said Robert. That's when she snapped out of it and remembers why she told Robert, he would have to use a rubber. "You fucked that skank, Robert!" Said Lashawn through, tears. "Yō sissy loving, high school sweetheart!" "Oh yeah?" Asks Robert. "Well, I fucked her, but I'm making love to you!" said Robert and enters Lashawn's Pussy!

CHAPTER TWENTY-NINE

Chapter 23

THE MOMENT OF TRUTH

The next morning, Lashawn felt kind of out of place and guilty. "For what? He is about to be my husband...I think!" said Lashawn. The whole act, that went down between her and Robert, was like for Robert. She got up and ran her some bath water and checked her phone. She seen where Jacorius had texted once and called once. He didn't leave a message. She felt guilty texting him, but she did. {Hey Jacorius! I'm sorry, I didn't show up. Hope you're not mad at me! I got caught up! When you get up, call me.} She knew that Jacorius might be up, so she would tarry around for a few minutes to see if he responds.

Jacorius was just rolling over and turning his phone on, when he seen he had a text from Lashawn. He opens it up and reads it. 'Didn't show up, cause you got caught up! Caught up doing what I wonder? It doesn't matter, I ain't tripping!" He texts her a brief message back. {Give me a minute.} Jacorius had a feeling that something wasn't right! When Lashawn didn't never get back at him, through texting or calling, he had kind of got out of his mind by staying somewhat busy at the club. He knew it was close to Lashawn's wedding, so she probably was handling some last-minute business. Or whatever! "May have been with her fiancé! Who knows." Said Jacorius to himself. He wanted Lashawn as a wifey, for real! But he'll take it how it comes. It's funny, because him and Lashawn both had fallen deeply in love with each other, but she was about to marry another man! Either she was very confused, a freak, who liked to have her cake and eat it too, or just straight slutty! Punching the pillow in his bed. He was mad at himself, because he let his feelings got involved. "Fuck it! I guess I'll just be her nigga, and he can be her man!" He got up and took a bath and got himself together, before he even called Lashawn back. "Hey!" Said Lashawn, as she answered the call. "What's up?" Asks Jacorius. "Oh nothing. Just sitting here at the office, trying to get a little work done. What up?" "Just cooling. Are you okay?" Asks Jacorius. A brief pause. "Yeah, I'm okay! Just a few rough spots. Confused, jittery... I don't know. Why you ask me that? You can tell?" "Yeah... I hear it in your voice." Said Jacorius. "Y'all going to stop, hearing stuff in my voice!" Giggled Lashawn. "Who is y'all?" "You and my friend." Said Lashawn, and then she started telling Jacorius about one of her girlfriends, recognizing that something was wrong, through her voice.

"I know you was wondering, where I was yesterday, when I didn't show up, to check your club out." "Yeah. I had called, but when you didn't get back at me, I felt like you might have been busy, or something." Said Jacorius. His instincts were telling him, that she was or might have been with Robert, but he wasn't going to say it though. To player for that! "Well. After I left Henrietta's, I went to the office for a minute and then I went home. And when I got there, Robert was there and.. We discussed some things, or whatever. Jacorius, I don't know what to do!" "Look... Baby just follow your heart. What do your instincts or that small voice tells you? Just follow that. Whatever, I'm here... But you know, the show must go on!" smoothly said Jacorius. Back in player mode! He had gathered that, Lashawn was confused, on what she really wanted to do. He wasn't going to pressure her. She wasn't a freak, nor a slut. So, that's where the conflict is at, roaring in the depths of her soul. Because her friend, in which she is to have the double wedding with, told her the same thing! Exactly what Jacorius had just told her. "Follow your heart." What Jacorius didn't know or at least what Lashawn thinks he don't know, is that her heart, mind, soul, and body is leaning more towards him! "But what he means by the show must go on?" Lashawn asked herself. Something else, in another corner of her mind said: "You know what he means! And that is, he's not going to put his life on hold for you." "Okay, okay." Said Lashawn. "You're the second person done told me, about following my heart!" "Oh yeah? Well, that's confirmation baby! But look, I'm about to go handle something. Then I'm going to the club, to see the finishing touches. Oh, I forgot to tell you the grand opening, going to be on the same day of your wedding! Well, that same night!" Now, Lashawn mind was reeling like crazy now.

"What!? Why are you going to do it that day?" "Well, it's time. I mean everything is straight! Dee-Dee and a couple of the girls done recruited, so many strippers who going to work there and is ready! Everything is set!" Excitedly said Jacorius. The wedding was in 3 days, that Saturday! Dread set in Lashawn's mind. "Okay Jacorius. How long are you going to be over there?" "I don't know. Probably all day!" "Okay... I'll come over there and check things out. Ain't no naked women, going to be walking around in there is it?" Asks Lashawn. "Nawl!" laughs Jacorius. "I'll call you and let you know when I'm coming." "Okay! That's what's up!" "Bye." Said Lashawn, in a sad tone, like she always does when they get off the phone or depart from each other. "Bye." said Jacorius. And they hung up. Lashawn really wanted to talk to Jacorius, a little longer and vent! Talk to him, just because! "Damn! I love this man." Said Lashawn, as she looked at a picture of him on her desk. The feeling was mutual, because as Jacorius hung up, he was thinking the same thing, as he was looking at a picture of Lashawn in his phone! It was a picture of Lashawn, in her hotel room, when her and her friends/ boss lady, Cornelius, went to an IT conference in Atlanta. "Damn I love this woman!" Said Jacorius. He was tempted to call her back, because he knew that she wanted and needed to talk to him! And he wanted and needed to talk to her! But he was going to hold off and see what was going to happen. Lashawn was at her desk, mind running a hundred miles per hour! All is on her mind is, what is she going to do. "Follow your heart!" Is all that is ringing in her mind. Lashawn proceeded to work, to ease her mind, from her current dilemma.

After about two-hours of none stop entering data, crunching numbers, and typing, Lashawn sat back in her chair and stretched, and closed her eyes closed. "Lashawn girl, are you okay?" Her eyes popped open, and she jumped at the same time. "Cornelius!" Laughs Lashawn. "Girl, you scared me!" "You scared me! Sitting there with your eyes closed!" Said Cornelius. "How much sleep you been getting girl?" Asks Cornelius, as she pulled a chair up and sat next to Lashawn. "Girl, you know how I sleep! Laughs Lashawn. "I'm getting better though. About five- six hours altogether." "Hmmm... Okay! But what else is bothering you? You know, I've been knowing you a long time. So, I know when something is bothering you. If it's none of my business, you don't have to tell me!" Said Cornelius. Cornelius is sort of a big sister, auntie figure, to Lashawn. She's been knowing Lashawn practically all of their life! "Well, life!" Said Lashawn. "Go on." Said Cornelius, edging Lashawn on to continue. "I mean... All that's going on! About to get married and I'm not..." "Sure, that you want to do it now." Said Cornelius, finishing Lashawn's sentence for her. Lashawn looked at Cornelius in a shocked way. "Girl don't look all surprised!" Said Cornelius. "I can imagine, or should I say, I've been there before." Lashawn was sitting there, kind of awestruck. "Yes, I have!" Said Cornelius. "Everything was going okay with us. Some flaws he had, I overlooked. When I should have been more analytical and objective about the flaws and base my decision to go ahead and marry, off of what my heart would have told me, after I had analyzed things! Cause, no matter what, my heart still was telling me to hold off! You're with me?" Asked Cornelius. "Yeah! I'm with you. Keep going." Said Lashawn.

"All I'm telling you is... Follow your heart, Lashawn. But remember. We only live once!" "People keep telling me to follow my heart!" "There you have it!" Said Cornelius. "I think I'm going to talk to my pastor." Said Lashawn. "What do your mother say about it?" Asked Cornelius. "Girl you better marry that man!" Said Lashawn, mocking her mother. Lashawn and Cornelius talked and laughed for a moment. About her divorce. And how it came about. Lashawn left work early to go and talk to her pastor and see what he has to say.

"This bitch going to be off the chain Jacorius!" said Brad, one of Jacorius's cousins from Alabama. Brad had been coming down to Florida buying exotic weed and pills from Jacorius. Jacorious had already told his cousin about his club, so he was down there, early for the grand opening! Him and a couple more of his cousins and homeboys from Alabama and Atlanta. "Yeah, it's going to be banging!" Said Jacorius, as he was looking at his Rolex, checking the time, and wondering was Lashawn coming through. "Damn cuz! Who are these hoes?" Said another one of his cousins from Alabama. When Jacorius looked up, it was Niecy and a couple of her home girls. All of them, had on some heels, red bones, tatted up, flexing with some type fitting clothes on. "Oh, that's Niecy. A broad I used to fuck with." said Jacorius. "What's up boo?" Said Niecy as she hugs Jacorius. "What's up boo!" Answers Jacorious. "Oh, let me introduce you and your friends to my folks." Jacorious introduced Niecy and her girlfriends to his cousins and homies. "Look, you going to give my partners a job?" Asks Niecy. "We already had some auditions last week Niecy." Said Jacorius, as he gave the girls an appraising look. "Cuz don't do them like that! Let them audition now!" said Jacorius's cousin Pat. "I mean if they don't mind." One of Jacorius partner, Chris agreed with Pat. Chris was going to be the manager of the club, so Jacorius didn't hesitate.

"Okay... There's a stage, and poles. "Hey Quinn turn the music on, so these girls can audition. One at a time!"

"Okay!" Said Quinn. Quinn was there making sure the DJ equipment was official, so he was already in the booth. The music came on. Wale's song, featuring T-Pain, Rick Ross and Meek Mills. "My girl bad, looking like a bag of money!" One of the girls immediately hit the stage and started performing. She was slowly taking off her clothes, dancing in a seductive way, as Jacorius and his cousins and friends, went to throwing money at the girl. By now the other three joined in! By now, they had a mini show going on. The DJ switched the music up to an up-tempo song by Ludacris, "Pussy popping on a handstand." They really were acting up now! Some of the other girls, who was just hanging around got involved, cause the guys who was present from the remodeling company, who was involved in remodeling and doing finishing touches to the club. The guys who were hanging around with Jacorius, all of them had money, in their pockets. A couple of lap dances was going on, pole work, a couple of girls had put all the way on, by doing the old dance, in chairs and the handstands! A P Poppin fest!

Lashawn mind was running everywhere, now that she has went and talked to her pastor. After talking to Cornelius, she went to the church to try and get some kind of confirmation. Everybody was telling her to follow her heart. "I wish Daddy was here! He would tell me what I needed to do. Or at least what I wanted to hear." Lashawn thought to herself. With the pastor told her, count her kind of threw her on a loop! "Lashawn... Maybe you're right where you're supposed to be!" Said the pastor. You need to pray about it. Lashawn was kind of feeling what the pastor was saying, but truly her heart wasn't all the way there. She called Jacorius, to let him know that she was coming, but she didn't get an answer. She was about to leave a message, changing her mind Lashawn hit the end button to hang the phone up. "I'm almost there anyway!" Said Lashawn, as she was driving a couple of blocks near the club.

Jacorius missed Lashawn's call. He was preoccupied, with the girls Niecy brought by getting a lap dance. Ole girl was giving it all she had, the way she was dancing in Jacorius lap, to R.Kelly's "Seems Like You're Ready." That's about the time Lashawn walked in. "Damn bitch! You just auditioning to work here at the club, not to see if you can fuck him through his clothes!" Said Niecy, as she smoked a blunt of Kush. "She just getting jealous now! I told her, if y'all couldn't work it out, let me have you!" Whispered the girl in Jacorius ear, as she was pulling on the back of the chair, he was sitting in. It appeared that she was trying to screw Jacorius through his jeans! Lashawn was appalled at what she was seeing. What in the world!?" Said Lashawn. She noticed Jacorius ex-girlfriend, was talking stuff, to the girl in Jacorius lap. "Bitch! Get up! He going to hire you. 'Damn! You doing too much! Get out of my man's lap!" Said Niecy, as she was pulling the girl by her arm. "Yō man?" Answers Lashawn under her breath. I think I better go!" said Lashawn to herself. Just as she was about to turn around and walk off, she met eyes with Niecy.

"Hey! You want to see him?" Asks Niecy, pointing at Jacorius. That's when he looked back and seen it was Lashawn. "Oh shit!" Said Jacorius, as he jumped up. Lashawn was already feeling out of place, the way she was dressed. Black slacks, black button down, to go with the slacks, and some 4-inch heels. Looking all professional like she's coming or going to an office. She didn't know whether to go on out the door or stay and talk to Jacorius. Actually, she was furious about what she just witnessed! She once told Jacorius, she was jealous about the women on Facebook, but now, if she ever was in doubt, about the way she really felt, that was gone! Cause indeed she was definitely jealous! "Hold up Lashawn!" Said Jacorius, walking toward Lashawn, feeling that she was about to leave. "What's up?" Asked Jacorius, as he walked up to Lashawn. "I thought you said no naked women." Said Lashawn, pointing towards the four women, who was putting their clothes on and talking loudly. "No, they were auditioning." Said Jacorius. "Dancing in your lap?" Said Lashawn, letting her mask fade away! Slightly showing her anger.

Jacorius cocked his head to one side like "What?" making Lashawn regain her composure. "I'm sorry! I called but you didn't answer and I..." "You're cool baby!" interrupted Jacorius. "What you just seen, was nothing! Nothing but an audition!" Slowly said Jacorius. "I just... Just kind of wilding out and let her give me a lap dance. Forgive me baby!" "You cool, you cool!" said Lashawn, grabbing Jacorius arm. "Show me around." Said Lashawn. Jacorius escorts Lashawn around the club, showing her around. He introduces her, to his cousins and friends from out of town. Niecy was standing there, with one hand on her hips, trying to look intimidating to Lashawn, who matched her stare! "Hey! We meet again." Said Lashawn and a cheerful but mocking tone. "Yeah... You again!" Said Niecy in a slow sarcastic way. Lashawn didn't care. Thinking about what she heard Niecy say, when she first walked in the club. "Get out of my man's lap!" Then Lashawn remembers, when she saw her on Jacorius arm, at the comedy club! Looking all conceited and ghetto glamorous! Now the tables had turned! And Lashawn was all up under Jacorius then! Jacorius peeping what's going on but not feeding into it. After he showed Lashawn around, they stood outside and talked.

"I don't mean to sound all jealous and out of place, but what is she doing here?" Asks Lashawn. "Who Niecy?" responds Jacorius. "Whatever her name is! Your ex!" Said Lashawn. "No, she brought those girls over, to get them a job and I told her about the auditions was last week. And that's when my cousin them, went to running their mouth, gassing things up! And that's when I let them put on!" "Okay." Said Lashawn. Lashawn told Jacorius she had just went and talked to her pastor and what they talked about. Jacorius just listened, as usual. "I don't know Jacorius." Said Lashawn. "Well, thanks for the tour of your establishment! It's nice!" "Thanks!" Said Jacorius as he leaned down in the car, to kiss Lashawn. She hesitated, only for a second or two and she kisses Jacorius as if it's their last kiss! "Call me." Said Lashawn, as Jacorius was walking off, heading back into the club. Lashawn pulled off.

Lashawn was overwhelmed now. She knew that she could not say anything about, what she saw at Jacorius's club, because she was about to marry a man! Hopefully. But how could she be with Jacorius and trust him, around all those naked women? All the time! She knew what he would say: "Strictly business! Nothing personal." "Get it out of your mind Shawn!" She said out loud in the car, as she drove home. It's 2 days before showtime. "Damn! Got to make my mind up."

Jacorius was up early Saturday morning, excited about the grand opening of his new strip club, "Royal Flush!" Everything was in place. He was kind of nervous, but he was going to work his way through it. He was happy and sad at the same time! Sad, because the day was Lashawn's wedding! But that was impossible! When he had done crossed the line and fell in love, with Lashawn and was ready to marry her himself! Lashawn told him where the wedding was taking place at. He was thinking about going, but he hadn't made his mind up just yet. The wedding was going to be at 2:00 p.m. His club was going to open tonight at 9:00 p.m. Jacorious didn't know, was he actually able to stand there and watch the wedding! He had so many mixed feelings about the situation. To ease his mind, Jacorius smoked a blunt, jumped in his truck and just rode around and reflected on what's been going on. "I wonder, why in the fuck she just didn't tell me!" Thinks Jacorius to himself. Lashawn waited till the last minute, to tell Jacorius that she was engaged to get married. If Jacorius would have known that he wouldn't have let his feelings got involved. He would have kept it player and just continue to fuck Lashawn! That was his style anyway! Get money and see how many women he can go through! Even with his own main lady, he would live like that, for situations in which he's in now! On to the next one If things don't work out. Plan B! The only thing about that, is Jacorius was feeling Lashawn so deeply, he had fixed in his mind to be faithful and just settle down. What got Jacorius disappointed in himself, is that he believed Lashawn, when she told him that, she wouldn't leave him in the dark!

That derived from a conversation they once had: "Okay Lashawn... You know you got my nose wide open! Don't have me in the dark, when it comes to your situation! Yo man or whatever!" "What you mean, have you in the dark?" Asked Lashawn. "Just what I said! Have me in the dark, like.. Ain't nothing to y'all, but it's about to be over and when the lights turn on, damn! There he is!" Lashawn laughed. "No, no, Jacorius, you won't have to worry about that!" "Don't have to worry about that and here it is, she about to marry the nigga!" Said Jacorius. After he played that old conversation back in his mind. "Well, shit happens!" And lo and behold Lashawn is texting him now!

"Girl, what is wrong with you?! You supposed to be one of the happiest girls on Earth right about now! You're sitting around like you're about to go to a funeral! Instead of a wedding!" Said one of her best friends from college, Deborah. "I came way down here from Birmingham; Alabama and you're sitting around like you're moping! You are about to elope!" "Girl, I know! I'm okay, I'm just... Just kind of nervous! I guess." Laughs Lashawn. "Well, I guess it's normal to have butterflies. But you are acting like it's more than butterflies! Like something is bothering you! And you keep messing with that phone! You have sent, how many texts out now? Three or four?" Asked Debra. In an almost exasperated way, Lashawn sat her phone down, on the coffee table and got up at the same time. "I'm okay!" Said Lashawn. Then walked off to the kitchen. "You want something to drink?" Asked Lashawn. "Like what? We don't need to be drunk, before the ceremony!" Said Deborah. At the refrigerator, Lashawn rolled her eyes. "No Deborah, I'm talking about some tea or something. You want some green tea?" "Whatever!" Said Debra. Lashawn got the tea out, grabs two glasses, put some ice in them and pours them both some tea.

She really wants to warm some tea up, to help her calm down and try hard to keep her mind, off of the man who makes her throb and ache in places she didn't know would do that! Just off of a conversation! She was getting antsy and kind of mad that Jacorius hadn't text her back. She really needs him bad right now! His voice is soothing to her. But if he didn't, Lashawn understood. It's her wedding day, he must be furious, then at the same time, is the grand opening of his strip club! "I hope he has text me back!" Mumbled Lashawn. As she walked back in the living room, with their tea. She handed Debra her glass and went and sat hers down and grabbed her phone, to see if she had a text from Jacorius. "I'm not in your business, but you must be looking for an important text!" Said Deborah. "Sort of!" Said Lashawn. "Girl, just relax!" Said Deborah, and she put her hand on Lashawn's knee. "Whatever it is, that's bothering you, I'm sure you'll get over it after you and Robert tie the knot!" "Maybe." Said Lashawn, as she leaned up and grabbed her phone, off of the coffee table again, to see had Jacorius text her back. No dice! He hadn't text her back. "This is crazy!" Said Lashawn as she almost threw her phone back down. "You're going to tell me what's crazy?" Asked Deborah. Letting out a nervous breath of air, Lashawn was very irritated! "Nothing, Deborah nothing! All the time, what was crazy to Lashawn, is how she was waiting on Jacorius to text her back and comfort her, and kind of coach her through this dilemma, when she was about to marry Robert, in the next couple of hours. Crazy!

Jacorius rode around for nearly an hour, ignoring his phone and just thinking. He pulled up to his club, to just go and walk through to admire his spot and visualize how things were going to jump tonight. Grabbing his phone, as he was exiting the truck, that's when he noticed the text from Lashawn. He read them, but didn't answer them. "Now she needs somebody to talk to!" Said Jacorius, as he unlocked the club and walked in. He actually felt bad for not texting Lashawn back. They made a promise to each other, to always have each other's back, no matter what! "I'll get at her later... Maybe a week or two from now! No, I might hit her up right before the wedding." Said Jacorius looking at his phone. "Damn! The wedding is in a couple of hours!" Jacorius was still thinking about going to the wedding. He walked around the club, doing a visualization exercise, so to speak. Picturing how he was going to be swaggering around the club. Looking at all the naked women doing their thing! Picturing all the money he was going to get off of the door, off of the liquor, beer, food, VIP. He walked to where his office was and sat down, and checked the monitors, to make sure everything was working. He checks the secret compartment where he keeps his pistols and rifles. Yeah, got to have that fire! He got up and checked exits and pictures how he would exit the building without nobody seeing him, being the always strategizing dude. "Everything going to be straight!' Said Jacorius. The club was about 30,000 square feet, with four stages, four bars, and was expecting about 100 to 150 strippers to be working and the rapper "2 Chains" was booked to perform at the grand opening! All Jacorius seen was money! And lots of it! Then like a vapor miss, the vision vanished momentarily. He thought about Lashawn and looked at his watch. "Fuck it! I'm going to her wedding." Jacorius closed everything down and quickly walks to his truck, to go take a bath and get ready to make his presence felt!

Lashawn was almost a nervous wreck, as time was counting down for the wedding. "Girl just be calm! Everything is going to be all right." said Debra, as they help Lashawn with her wedding dress and a little makeup. "Mama, you are looking so pretty!" Said Lashawn's oldest daughter. "Thanks!" Said Lashawn. Her daughter kind of knew what was going on with her mother. Lashawn had talked with her about it, partially. She didn't really tell her everything about her and Jacorius, being involved. But she told her enough, for her to know that her mother wasn't all the way into Robert anymore to marry him. "So why are you still going through with it?" Asks her daughter. "I don't know! I am confused baby!" Said Lashawn. "Confused? Okay Mama. Terrica was so mad, thinking about you marrying Robert, that she was crying the other night." "Why?" Asked Lashawn. She was definitely all ears when it came to her baby. "Because she was reflecting on the times, when it seemed like he doesn't really care about you. Like when you had that surgery and he was acting like he didn't want to go get your prescription filled, you were in pain and at the same time didn't want to let nobody get your meds!" Lashawn sat there listening and thinking about what her daughter was talking about. And the only response she had was, "everything will be okay. I promise you! It will get better." "I know Mama!" said her daughter as they hug. After making last minute preparations and polishing up, it was only minutes now, before the wedding!

"Y'all girls ready?' Asks Deborah, referring to Lashawn and Jenetta, who was to be married at the same time, and the flower girls. "Yeah, I guess so!" Nervously said Lashawn, and Jenetta. Jenetta's father was there escort her, to the altar and Lashawn's god brother was there to escort her. Everyone filed out in order, like it was supposed to go. The Organ player played, here comes the bride! Cameras flash, camera phones were in the air, recording and snapping shots. Video cameras rolled. The photographer, in which was hired, was doing his thing. At the altar, there stood the preacher and the groom. Everything seemed like it was in slow motion to Lashawn, as everything which have took place in her life, in the last two years or three years flashed her mind!

Jacorius was already running late, purposely. So, he kind of speeded up a little bit, as he finished smoking a blunt! "Damn! The wedding almost done started." Said Jacorius, checking the time, as he weaved through traffic in his drop Jag. He was thinking to himself, how would things be with Lashawn, now that she is married? Would he give her some space? Would he turn it up a notch, just for the sport of it? Or will he just remain her friend and just be there for her, when she needs him? And when she needs her some? "I'll just play it by ear! Living for the moment!" Said Jacorius. Pulling up to the church, Jacorius was getting butterflies, for some reason! Like he was about to get married! He noticed the parking lot was full up and down the road, both sides were full of cars. Jacorius found him a parking spot to park, down the street from the church. He jumped out of the car, checked his self in the mirror and off of the glossy candy paint on his car, and he walked off. Jacorius was sharp as a tack! He had on an all-white Prada linen suit, with some all-black Prada shoes, Louis Vuitton frames, diamond earrings, gold Rolex, embedded with princes and baguettes diamonds. A 26-in diamond chain, and to top it off, he had his dreads plaited together, in 7-8 big locks! As Jacorius approached the church's door, he heard the music just stopping, so he knew she was at the altar! Time for the moment of truth!

Lashawn and Jenetta were looking so gorgeous, as they were just stepping to the altar. Both couples were smiling. Smiling, was so much part of Lashawn's demeanor, that if something was wrong with her, or something was so heavy on her mind, bothering her, a person wouldn't really be able to tell just by looking at her! She was wearing her mask strong, when the preacher started talking. Looking in Robert's eyes. "We are gathered here today..." That's when something told Lashawn, to play it off, but look towards the door. Following her intuition, she looks towards the door and almost fainted! Lashawn had to do a double take. "What the hell?" Lashawn mumbled to herself. Robert picked up on it! So, he looked too. He didn't really know what she was looking at. Was it someone in the crowd or what. "Wait a minute!" Thought Robert to his self as he calmly looks back to her, and the door, he noticed this short stocky guy, with some big, long plaits or dreads had just stepped in, standing in the back. "He looks familiar!" Robert thought to himself. That's when he remembered dude.

He had those stripper girls, who was at the bachelor party. Jacorius had come through for a moment, talking to one of the girls, on the business style and left. Oh yeah? It was the one named Dee-Dee. Robert had already met Jacorius before then, a while back when he was doing some heavy tricking, with one of the call girls, who worked for the escort service. He had fell in love with her and somehow found out where the office was and was coming through looking for the girl and acting like they were on some super personal shit! Jacorius could have cared less, but he was kind of spooking the girls, who was working the office most of the time. So that's when Jacorius stepped in. Nevertheless, Robert didn't pay him much mine, but his presence made him kind of leery! Not knowing, was he there on some type of putting Robert's business on the glass or what? When Robert looked at Jacorius, Jacorius recognized him off the top! "Damn! She is marrying that trick ass nigga!?" Said Jacorius to himself. That's the dude, who had the bachelor party last night and the same dude I had to talk to about hounding Deandra! About to draw unwanted attention to Jacorius's escort service, with that stalking type of action.

"Oh well!" Said Jacorius in his mind. He knew that Lashawn had seen him, when she did a double take and bucked her eyes! Now things have escalated to another level, now that Jacorius is at the wedding. Lashawn Mind is running in high gear. The scales of justice have illuminated itself, within Lashawn's spirit. She's weighing her situation up, which is now taking place. Then she's weighing up the two men! on the balances. Jacorius and Robert. Hands down Jacorius wins and outweighs Robert in her spirit. Now she's wondering, what in the world is she doing up here! Robert was talking, doing the ceremony, of exchanging their vows, but to Lashawn it all is sounding like the teacher on Charlie Brown. Everything is back in slow motion. Lashawn thought that she could handle Jacorius being there, but now she knows the truth! The reverend was clearing his throat, to snap Lashawn out of her daze. "Lashawn." "Oh... Umm." Just as she was about to continue, she looked out in the audience, towards the door, where Jacorius was still standing, with his Louis V shades in his hands. Looking at Lashawn, feeling her attention and vibes that she's giving off! Lashawn looks back at Robert as she starts to frown.

"Take your time." Said the preacher. "I'm sorry. I... She looks back at Jacorious, he smirks at her, lifts his head up at her beckoning her to come on. Saying: "Come on." with his mouth at the same time! "I... Can't do this!" That's when Jacorius was putting his shades back on and turning and leaving out the church and Lashawn took off from the altar, heading towards the door, behind Jacorius! "Lashawn! Lashawn!" Hollered Robert. Jenetta had her hands over her mouth and her soon to be husband, was shaking his head! The preacher was standing there, mouth and eyes wide open, stuck with shock! Robert was stuck with the shock, embarrassment, and anger! Then he got in motion. He walked off the altar down the aisle, and out the door. Lashawn's mother, sister, and brother was there looking around. "Umm, Mama, what just happened? asked Lashawn's brother. Jacorius was down the street, walking towards his car, as it started raining all of a sudden.

Lashawn had busted out of the door of the church, ran down the steps, looking both ways! Then she spotted him. "Jacorius." Screams Lashawn. "Damn! She came on for real! I can't believe she did it!" said Jacorius, as he turned around and started walking towards Lashawn. She was running towards him. At first, he was walking, then he started slowly running towards Lashawn. When they met, she jumped in his arms, like a little girl, wrapping her thighs around his waist! He caught her and they immediately kissed, like they've been missing each other and hadn't seen each other in months or years! "Lashawn!" Hollers Robert, not believing his eyes, as his fiancé, passionately kisses another man, in the rain! "I know you fucking hear me!" Jacorius let her down, as they stop kissing. She looks back at Robert, as he stood there angry, breathing like a bull! "No Robert! I don't hear you. You were never hearing me!" Said Lashawn.

"I'm sorry... Let's go Jacorius!" Said Lashawn as she grabs Jacorius by the arm and headed toward his car. "So, you going to do me like this Lashawn? You going to leave me at the altar, for some sleazy ass wanna be pimp? That guy runs an escort service Lashawn! He manages strippers and sell drugs!" Jacorious almost had enough. So, he stopped and looked back at Robert, as Robert continues to walk towards them, screaming obscenities. "Come on Jacorius. Look over him!" Said Lashawn as she was getting in the car. Jacorius went ahead and opened the driver's door and was about to get in the car, that's when Robert grabs Jacorius arm and instantly, Jacorius was pulling his pistol with one hand and knocks Robert's hand off of his arm with the other. "Shawn you better get this nigga!" Said Jacorius. "Noo!" screamed Lashawn, as she jumped out of the car. "Robert please go! It's over with okay!"

Said Lashawn, as she got between the men. "It's over!" Screaming Lashawn. "Please go Robert and understand, it's over, it's a wrap! I hate that it went this far! I'm sorry for that, But..." By then Robert had cocked back and swung on Lashawn, but the lick hadn't landed, because Jacorius had caught Robert's arm and slapped him down, with the butt of the gun and stood over him cocking his pistol at the same time, pointing it in Robert's face! "Nigga you at the right place to die!" Said Jacorius. "Please Jacorius no! Don't do it! Let him go and let's go!" Screamed Lashawn. A crowd had filled out of the church and was watching the drama. A couple of women screamed! Robert's best man and a couple of his friends ran to his side and helped him up. As Jacorius slowly backed up to his car, with Lashawn pulling him back. "Please let's go!" Lashawn cried. Snapping Jacorius out of his zone. "Okay get in the car." Said Jacorius. Lashawn ran around to the passenger side and Jacorius got in the car. Still looking at Robert and his friends, as he was about to pull off. Jacorius couldn't help it; he rolls the window down and told Robert: "I guess you'll listen now. But it's too late...Partner!" And pulled off.

CHAPTER THIRTY

Chapter 24

After the fiasco at the wedding, Jacorius and Lashawn rode up to Flagler's Beach, to Lashawn's duck-off spot. Jacorious nicknames it the cave. Time, they step foot in the house, they were all over each other! Leaving a trail of clothes. Jacorius linen suit and Lashawn's wedding gown. Without any words being said, they made love off and on for hours! Jacorius and Lashawn laid within each other arms, listening to the rain outside. Both of their phones were going off, like at a telethon for Jerry's kids! "Why did you come?" Asks Lashawn. "Why did I come? Baby I couldn't help it! I mean your loving... That thing snatching down there! Lashawn caught on to what Jacorius was saying, and she punched him in the side. "I mean the wedding!" 'Oh! I couldn't stop thinking about you. I'm sorry if I ruined everything for you." Said Jacorius. "It's all right! It wasn't meant to be anyway. I was indecisive about it from the jump! Then. When you showed up... I was wondering, what I was doing standing up there!" "You for real?" Asked Jacorius. Lashawn looked at him like he was crazy. "What happened and where am I now?" Asked Lashawn. "Okay, Okay Ms. smarty. I was just being modest." Said Jacorius. Both of their phones went off at the same time. They just looked at each other.

Then something dawns on both of them, and they both jumped up and grabbed their phones. Lashawn knew her daughters and her family was worried about her and Jacorius knew, that in a couple of hours, the grand opening of his club was about to go down! Lashawn answered hers and it was her daughter's. "Yeah, yeah, I'm okay!" Said Lashawn. "Robert was talking about signing a warrant on that guy, you left with, and..." "A warrant? I know he's not, when he's the one grabbed Jacorius and raised his hand to hit me!" Said Lashawn. "I know Ma! I think he changed his mind. He came home and packed his stuff and left!" "That's good for him baby!" Said Lashawn, as she continues to talk to her daughter. Jacorius was on the phone with his people. "Yeah... I'll be there in an hour, I already have, everything straight. I'll holler at y'all then." Said Jacorius, hanging up and answering other calls. Once both of them had answered all of their calls and returned calls, Jacorius jumped up and put on his clothes. "Oh, you got your grand opening tonight!" Said Lashawn. "Yeah... You are coming?" "After today's events, let me chill, okay?" "I feel you baby!! I'll catch up with you later on tonight... Or tomorrow morning." Said Jacorius. "Okay... Oh... You better not be down there getting no lap dances! I'm serious!" Said Lashawn. "I got you baby!" Said Jacorius, as he exited the house. Lashawn went and took a long bath, drunk a glass of wine, and reflected on everything what was taking place. When she got out of the tub, she talked on the phone to her mother, God brothers, God sisters, everybody who wanted to know what was going on! She filled them in on what was going on and let everyone interesting know, that she had crossed a line, in which was too hard to cross back over! In fact, it wasn't even an option, because she was happy and didn't care who didn't like it!

Epilogue

A year later, after the Botched wedding of Lashawn and Robert, Jacorius and Lashawn were at the altar! Ironic? Nah, this is what both of them wanted. As the preacher was going through the ceremony, Jacorius and Lashawn was looking in each other eyes, smiling. Jacorius, for a brief moment, was thinking, what if Lashawn leaves him at the altar, like she did Robert. But that thought quickly evaporated, like mist! Jacorius had truly handled his business with Lashawn. He knew how to love a woman! Especially a good woman like Lashawn. The question had surfaced before: "Would you have affair on me?" Coming from both parties. No was the answer. Jacorius knew why Lashawn crossed the line, on Robert. For one, Robert had already violated the code, over and over again! And she found out, instead of trying to do better, he got worse! By showing that he didn't genuinely care for his woman. Just because, a person says: If she cheats on him, she'll cheat on you! If she'll leave him, she'll leave you! Yeah, if Jacorius start lacking, in his responsibilities, in showing Lashawn that he cares deeply about her and for her. Stop showing the feelings of affection and romance and oh attentiveness, your woman might cross a line, in which she really doesn't want to cross, looking for someone who knows how to. A man like Jacorius. And me!

The End!

www.ingramcontent.com/pod-product-compliance
Lightning Source LLC
Chambersburg PA
CBHW060344310726
48976CB00003B/719